"Don't patronize me!" Trista snapped

"Sorry." Pierce drew up in front of her house. "It's a bit difficult to treat an adolescent femme fatale like a mature woman."

Trista's breath hissed between her teeth. Delivered in a cool, considering tone, his remark had been deliberate and calculated.

"As difficult as believing that a pompous cold-blooded lawyer with an inflated ego could be hiding a real man. You probably can't even kiss a woman without cross-examining her first and passing judgment afterward."

She got out of the car and slammed the door. But Pierce caught up to her before she reached the house. His hands grasped hers and swung her around. "If you wanted to be kissed that badly, Trista," he said, "all you had to do was ask me nicely."

DAPHNE CLAIR, a fourth-generation New Zealander, lives with her family of five in the subtropical area known as "The Winterless North." In addition to her contemporary romances, she writes poetry, historical novels under various names and has won literary prizes for her short stories. About three times a year she tutors courses to help other writers develop their craft. She says she hates windy days, shopping, daylight savings time, prickly plants and having her photograph taken.

Books by Daphne Clair

Don't miss any of our special offers. Write to us at the following address for information on our newest releases.

Harlequin Reader Service
901 Fuhrmann Blvd., P.O. Box 1397, Buffalo, NY 14240
Canadian address: P.O. Box 603,
Fort Erie, Ont. L2A 5X3

DAPHNE CLAIR

the wayward bride

Harlequin Books

TORONTO • NEW YORK • LONDON
AMSTERDAM • PARIS • SYDNEY • HAMBURG
STOCKHOLM • ATHENS • TOKYO • MILAN

Harlequin Presents first edition June 1990
ISBN 0-373-11271-8

Original hardcover edition published in 1989
by Mills & Boon Limited

CHAPTER ONE

'CONGRATULATIONS, Pierce. A tricky case, that—you did well for our client.'

Geoffrey Vandeleur rose from behind the big desk and held out a hand to his younger colleague, his heavy-featured face wearing a pleased smile.

Pierce Allyn accepted the hand and gripped it briefly in his own long fingers. 'Thank you. I must admit I didn't know if the jury would wear the reduction of the charge from attempted murder to causing grievous bodily harm. It did seem like a somewhat premeditated attack.'

'But you showed the court that the victim had been in the habit of using violence against his family, and the woman's father was desperate to protect his daughter. You gained the sympathy of the jury with your defence. Personally, I think their decision to convict on the lesser charge was a fair one. Let's hope the judge gets the message and keeps the sentence within the spirit of the verdict.'

'The accused does have some previous convictions,' Pierce said. 'That will count against him.'

'Hmm. Well, you've done your part. Tell you what,' he added, moving from the desk to the bookcase against a side wall, 'we'll celebrate with a small drink.' He took a half-bottle of whisky from a cupboard set into the shelves, and in turning knocked over a framed photograph.

Pierce bent to pick it up, turning it over. 'No damage,' he said, checking the glass and frame.

'My daughter.' Geoffrey placed two glasses on his desk and began to uncork the bottle. 'Lovely, isn't she?' he added with pride.

Politely Pierce held the photograph a few moments longer. It was of a teenage girl with hazel eyes and a cloud of light brown hair, not quite blonde, smiling at the camera. 'She's very pretty,' he said, secretly amused at the older man's obvious infatuation with his offspring. 'Do you have other children?' He replaced the photograph and turned to accept the glass Geoffrey was holding out for him.

'No, she's the only one. Her mother died when she was only three years old. And—I didn't want to marry again.'

'I'm sorry.' Pierce appraised his senior with covert interest. He would never have thought Geoffrey Vandeleur would be a sentimentalist.

'Well, never had time, really,' Geoffrey said briskly, and raised his glass. 'Here's to your first case for our firm, and may all the others be as successful.'

As he finished the whisky, Pierce realised he was being subjected to a rather appraising look himself.

'Have we sent you an invitation to my daughter's party?' asked Geoffrey.

Surprised, Pierce shook his head. 'I don't expect——'

'I'll send you one. It's her twenty-first. Big day for her.'

'Thank you, but as your daughter doesn't know me, I don't know if she'd want——'

'I'd like to have you there.' Geoffrey was as tall as Pierce, their eyes on a level. His bland gaze held a hint of steel. 'It's time she met some worthwhile young men. I don't care much for the fellow she's been seeing lately. Not impressed with most of her friends, in fact. Told her the other day: at twenty-one it's time to stop behaving like an adolescent and think about her future. She's got her degree. Well, it doesn't hurt for a girl to have an education. Although how she managed to get through university, with all the gallivanting she does——' He stopped and gripped Pierce's arm briefly. 'But I won't bore you with this. Come along on the fifteenth and meet her anyway.'

'The boss trying to marry you off to his daughter already?'
Pierce's younger sister asked, when he told the story over a
family lunch the following weekend at his parents' home
north of Auckland. 'You must be popular!'

Pierce looked at her across the table, his grey eyes
amused. 'He was pleased with me at the time. But he didn't
actually suggest I should marry the brat.'

'Pierce!' his mother chided.

'How do you know she's a brat?' Charlotte, generally
called Charley, demanded.

Her older sister intervened, looking up from cutting her
two-year-old son's vegetables into pieces. 'Use your head,
Charley. He can't wait to marry her off to the first half-way
decent male who comes along . . .'

'Thank you, Antonia,' Pierce interjected.

Unlike Charley, Antonia had always insisted on being
given her full name. She grinned at him. 'That's OK.'

'I think Pierce would be quite a good catch,' Charley said.
'All my girlfriends flip over him. Tall, dark, handsome . . .'

'Charley,' Pierce said affably, 'shut up, will you?'

'If you do marry her——'

'Charley!'

'Well, you'll be going to the party, won't you?' She
smiled at him, her eyes innocent.

'I suppose so. I can't very well get out of it.'

Trista Vandeleur was even prettier in the flesh, with her
hair, fairer than in her photo, styled in loose curls brushing
her bare shoulders, and wearing a quite startling red dress
that didn't hug her figure so much as skim it, but still
managed to leave precious little to the imagination. She was
rather thinner than he had expected, although there was
nothing wrong with her shape, and in spite of the obvious

sophistication of the dress, which she wore with total confidence, she looked younger than twenty-one. He would have guessed, given the chance, perhaps eighteen.

Introduced by her father, Pierce handed over a gift-wrapped package containing a very expensive perfume which Charley had bought on his behalf, and was amused by the way she greeted him, politely holding out her hand, and giving him a look that said quite plainly, Oh, another stuffy junior partner from Daddy's office. How soon can I get away?

There was a faint flicker of interest when he smiled at her, saying, 'Congratulations. Thank you for allowing your father to invite me.'

She withdrew her hand from his. 'You didn't need to bring a present.'

'My younger sister assures me that you'll like it.'

'I'm sure I will.'

An older woman, perhaps an aunt, came up beside her out of the crowd that had already arrived. 'Another present, dear? Let me take it and open it for you.'

A burst of laughter came from a group of young people in a corner of the big room. The house was modern and very large, but already some of the rooms seemed to be overflowing. Trista looked past Pierce's shoulder, her hands moving to relinquish the package.

Pierce said, 'My sister would insist on opening all her presents herself.'

She brought her gaze back to him. 'How old is your sister, Mr Allyn?'

'Twenty.'

She looked at him with a hint of surprise, and he answered the unspoken question. 'I'm twenty-nine. Charley was a late baby.'

Her father said, 'Are you going to open that? The Bridgemans have just arrived.'

'Yes,' she said, and began peeling back the tape holding the stiff paper. Her fingernails were pale pink. He was surprised she hadn't painted them to match her dress, as she had her lips.

The glass bottle, held in a nest of satin, emerged from the wrapping. 'It's a new brand,' she said. 'I've never tried it.' She handed the torn paper to the woman at her side, and unstopped the bottle, touching it to her wrist, then sniffed. 'Mmm. Your sister was right.'

'I'm glad. May I . . .?' He caught her hand as she was about to lower it, and bent his head to her wrist. The scent reminded him of carnations with a spicier, slightly musky undertone, but not heavy.

She took away her hand rather suddenly, and he raised his head to find her eyes on him, rather wide and with a look of confused surprise in them. Again he thought she seemed younger than her age, and reminded himself that she was only just twenty-one.

An older couple came up to them and, before turning to greet them, Geoffrey said, 'Get yourself a drink from the bar, Pierce—over there.'

Pierce smiled at Trista again, and walked away.

He circulated, meeting a few people he knew, and many that he didn't. There seemed to be more of Trista's father's generation than of her own. But what the younger set lacked in numbers they made up for in presence, getting louder and more hilarious as the evening progressed and they downed more drinks. Towards midnight they were dancing on the wide terrace outside a pair of sliding glass doors, to a tape-recorded rock band playing at top decibel level. Trista, in her red dress, had her hands raised above her head, her hips swaying in time to the music, the light from the outside lamps shimmering on the shiny material as she moved, laughing at her partner and tossing her hair back with a shake of her head.

There was a swimming pool on the other side of the terrace, lit but unoccupied. It was autumn, and although the night was quite pleasant the water would be a little cool.

A shower of rain suddenly came spitting down on the patio, and the dancers scattered and ran for the house, squealing and laughing. Trista stood for perhaps three seconds with her arms wide and her face raised to the rain, and then, when her partner turned back for her, she ran too, losing a shoe before she made it inside. Her dancing partner scooped it up and followed her. She had sparkling beads of water caught in her curls, and as she turned, smiling, her eyes shining, Pierce saw the look of admiration and desire on the young man's face. Holding the shoe aloft, he grinned teasingly and, when she grabbed for it, clasped her waist, so that her body curved close to his.

'Pay me for it, then, the young man taunted, and swooped to kiss her, pressing his mouth on hers.

Her hands came down to push against his chest, giving him a silent shove away. Her eyes blazed for a moment, and he looked suddenly uncertain. Then she was laughing again, holding out her hand. 'All right, Pete, give it up. I've paid my forfeit.'

Pete smiled, relieved. 'OK, Cinderella,' he said. And he went down on one knee to fit the shoe back on her foot.

There were droplets of water running over her shoulders and she said, 'I'd better go and dry myself.'

On her way to the door, her glance met Pierce's slightly narrowed gaze. He smiled, and she blinked and then gave him a tiny smile back.

There had been food available all night, but as soon as Trista arrived back the three-piece band that had been playing in the main room where some of the older people were dancing played a drum-roll, and a large, elaborately iced cake was wheeled in.

Geoffrey made a conventional speech, mercifully short, and then Trista thanked her guests and cut the cake, to the usual chorus of song and cheers and some teasing from her young friends, before it was borne away to be cut into pieces and served to the guests.

Pierce wandered out on to the terrace. The rain had stopped, but the tiles were still wet and there was no one about. The night had turned cooler, but with his jacket on he was quite comfortable. He walked around the pool and discovered a pathway at the other side leading to a small gazebo in the shadow of bushes and tall trees. The house had been built on the site of an earlier one, and the garden must have been established fifty years ago or more. The noise from the party was muted. He went into the gazebo, and found it dry inside. A wooden bench ran around three sides, and he sat where he could look out through the arched doorway, catching glimpses of the people in the house through a gap in the shrubs as they crossed his view like distant figures on a stage.

He had developed a slight headache. Soon he could go home without seeming bored with the whole thing. Meantime it was pleasant here, and certainly no one would miss him in that crowd.

He closed his eyes and leaned back against the unpainted wall behind his head. After perhaps ten minutes, he became aware of two voices which were closer than the house, one male and one female. They were talking quietly, almost whispering, and then the woman's voice said clearly, '*No*, I said!'

Soft footfalls and the rustling of bushes followed, and then the girl was standing in front of the doorway, a few feet away. Her slim figure in the red dress was outlined against the light from the house.

Her companion joined her, stretching out a hand to take her by the arm. Pierce saw that this didn't seem to be Peter of the Prince Charming complex. 'You *are* a tease!' he said angrily.

'I wouldn't believe the guys when they told me, but it's true. You could drive a man crazy, Trista!'

'A *man*?' The scorn in her voice was deliberate. She laughed.

The hand dropped from her arm. He called her a name that made Pierce, watching from the darkness of the gazebo, lift his brows. 'One day,' he said passionately, 'you'll meet a guy who can handle you. And I hope I'm around to see it! I'd like to see you fall really hard for someone who'd treat you the way you've treated me.'

'When it happens,' she said, 'I'll send you a postcard.'

'Don't you *ever* take anything seriously, Trista?'

'Life's too short.'

'I'm in *love* with you!' The despair in his voice almost made Pierce wince. 'I don't just want to—to sleep with you——'

'I know *that*!'

'I mean——'

'Yes, why not say it? What's wrong with a good old Anglo-Saxon verb?'

'That's *not* what I meant!'

Trista turned away from him, looking towards the house. 'This conversation is getting very boring.'

'I'm trying to propose to you, Trista!'

She twisted again to face him. 'Propose—what?'

'What the hell do you think? Marriage, of course!' Pierce could see the slight lift of his shoulders as he took a deep breath. 'Will you marry me?'

She was silent, and Pierce couldn't see the expression on her face. Then she said abruptly, 'No. Sorry.'

'Is that all you've got to say?'

'What else can I say?' she asked carelessly. 'The answer's no. And I'm sorry.'

'No, you're not. You're not in the least sorry. This is what you've been bloody well angling for, isn't it? Get me down on my knees——'

'You're not, actually.'

'—and then kick me in the teeth. I'm not the first, am I? Just the latest in a long line of poor idiots who've fallen for you.'

'I can't help that.'

'Don't make me laugh! The way you look at a man, the way you dress—everything about you screams, "come and get it, fellers". You're a *cheat*, Trista. You promise but you don't deliver, do you? Why did you come out here with me if you didn't want me?'

'You *said*,' she reminded him, ' "let's walk outside for a while, and cool off." '

'He gave a derisive snort of laughter. 'Oh, come *on*. You're not that innocent. You knew what I wanted.'

'Why didn't you tell me?' she taunted. 'Something like, "Come into the garden, Trista, and let me maul you about and *enjoy myself* making you do what I want." It would have been more honest.'

'You were enjoying it, too!' he said hotly. 'At first.'

She was looking at the pool, but she tilted her head towards him then, and said softly and with the utmost contempt, 'How the hell would you know?'

Careful, girl, Pierce thought, as he saw the tension in the young man's body.

'I'll prove it!' The man lunged at her and she slapped him, but he kept coming. '*I'll show you*!' he said. 'I'll make you follow through for once.'

Pierce got to his feet, but even as he swiftly moved forward and his hand went to the man's shoulder, he heard a grunt of pain and the fellow doubled over, gasping.

Trista stepped back, her head whipping up to look at Pierce.

'Are you all right?' he said.

'Yes.' She went towards the doorway of the gazebo, and Pierce looked at the young man, slowly straightening now, breathing raggedly, even as he gasped, 'The bitch. The little bitch.'

'Time you went home, I think,' Pierce suggested pleasantly.

'I—she——' He came forward, and Pierce shifted slightly to stand in front of him. 'Yes,' he said, not without some sympathy. 'I know. Home, don't you think?'

After a while the younger man nodded, and walked slowly towards the house.

The girl was leaning against the frame of the doorway to the gazebo, her hands behind her. Her pose looked utterly seductive, and he felt a spasm of irritation. Then he saw how one hand was clutching the wood, and his gaze lifted quickly to her face. There wasn't much light, but just then the moon came scudding out of the clouds overhead. For a moment her features were sharply defined, and he saw that the curls and the make-up disguised a surprising bone-structure that hinted at a hidden strength of character when she was not smiling.

'Thank you,' she said, 'but I can look after myself.'

'So I noticed.'

'Where did you come from?'

'I was in the gazebo.'

Her head lifted. 'All the time?'

When he nodded, she said, 'You must have had an interesting time.'

He leaned on the opposite side of the doorway, looking down at her. 'Yes,' he said. 'It was—instructive.'

'I asked for it, didn't I?' She straightened suddenly. 'That's what you're thinking.'

'How would you know what I think?'

'You're a man, aren't you?' Turning her back to him, she started walking towards the pool.

He was just behind her when she reached it. 'Do you dislike men?' he asked her.

She faced him. 'Good heavens, no! I think men are—fun.'

'Cats,' he said, 'think mice are fun, don't they?'

'Cats think mice are food,' she shot back. 'You're a barrister, aren't you?'

'Yes.'

'Then you should know better than to believe one side of the story without hearing the other.'

Quite gently, he said, 'I'm not judging you, Trista.'

She stared up at him. 'Aren't you?'

He shook his head. 'But I noticed you didn't deny what he said.'

'What would be the use? Anyway . . .' Her voice trailed off.

'Yes?' he prompted.

She shrugged. 'Nothing. Do you want to dance?'

He could see her mood had changed. He had also seen that it took an effort of will. 'Yes,' he said. 'Inside.'

'The terrace is wet, anyway,' she said, and went ahead of him into the house.

The band was playing more modern music now, and the small area of dance-floor was almost completely taken up by the younger guests. The crowd had thinned considerably; quite a number of the older ones must have gone home.

They started dancing a few feet apart, like the others, and he saw the flicker of surprise in her eyes. He didn't dance often but he had a good sense of rhythm, and Charley kept him up the with latest moves. He watched Trista, and, although she was smiling, after a few moments her eyes took on a remote look, and he had the impression that she had distanced herself in some way, withdrawn to some inward place where only the music and the movements of her body were real to her.

Then the band stopped, and she gave him a strangely blind smile, as though she wasn't quite sure who he was.

It was nearly one o'clock. The band leader said, 'Last

dance, people,' and there were moans from around the floor, and cries of, 'Slack, eh?'

Trista raised her arms and said loudly, 'We don't have to stop just because they're packing up! We've got plenty of tapes. I want to dance all night—it's my birthday!'

Her friends cheered and whooped, and as the music started again they began gyrating with renewed energy.

Trista tossed back her hair and started moving her hips and shoulders, her smile wide and her eyes sparkling with laughter.

Then the tempo of the music slowed, and she looked full into Pierce's eyes and moved closer, sliding her arms about his neck. He looked down at the blatant challenge in her eyes and smiled slightly as he put his arms about her waist and fitted her snugly into his body. Someone found a light switch and dimmed it.

'You're a good dancer,' she said, still looking up into his face, her head thrown back.

'You, too,' he answered. 'Where do you go to?'

She blinked. 'I'm right here.'

'*Now* you are.' His arms tightened fractionally as if to remind her.

'Well, then . . .' She shrugged.

'You know what I mean.'

She looked away, then rested her head against his shoulder. 'Let's not talk.'

They danced in silence until the band finished with a flourish, and the other couples began to drift off. But Trista didn't move out of his arms. Looking up at him again, she said, 'Will you stay? We'll be dancing for hours yet.'

That poor bloke never had a chance, he thought, gazing into her flawless face. She really was enough to make any man's head spin. In fact, his own headache seemed to have disappeared. He shook his head. 'Sorry, I have a heavy case coming up. Got to work tomorrow.'

Her face suddenly closed. She dropped her arms and moved back out of his hold. 'Fine,' she said, with a lift of her head. 'Good luck with the case.'

He said gravely, 'Thank you.' He wondered if she had ever suffered the slightest rejection before. On impulse, he put a hand under her chin so that he could see her face. Her lips were no longer painted bright red, only a smudge of colour remaining. Her mouth looked both inviting and vulnerable. 'Happy birthday, Trista,' he said, and kissed her lightly. 'Goodnight.'

He saw Geoffrey in the doorway of the room as he turned away. The older man had an air of complacency. 'Leaving already?' he asked, when Pierce thanked him for the evening. 'The young ones aren't going home yet. I expect we'll be giving them breakfast.'

'I'm not quite as young as they are.' Pierce smiled. 'And I have some work to do on the Pendleton case.'

'Ah, well.' Geoffrey put a hand on his arm. 'Come again some time. For dinner.'

'Thank you very much.'

'Trista's taken a fancy to you, eh?'

For a moment Pierce almost expected him to wink. 'I wouldn't say that, exactly,' he answered. 'She's being a good hostess, I think. Making sure the guests enjoy themselves.'

'Don't underestimate yourself. Although she is a good little hostess—when she puts her mind to it. One thing she does love is a party.'

Along Tamaki Drive, the road was wet and slick, the pohutukawas lining the road on the sea side dipping and waving. Out on the black harbour a few lights made long, wavy lines in the water, and on the Harbour Bridge shaped the arches of its structure. Pierce could hear the hiss of water under the car wheels as another shower forced him to turn on his windscreen wipers. He recalled the raindrops caressing Trista's bare shoulders, and shook his head. 'A brat,' he said softly, and laughed. Her lips had been soft and surprised, and rather sweet. Deceptive, he thought. The girl shows all the signs of being a heartless little trollop. But the kiss had been prompted by a strange impulse to comfort.

CHAPTER TWO

TRISTA'S reflection gazed back at her critically. She wasn't sure if she liked her hair up. Usually if she wanted it out of the way she tied it back in a ponytail. But tonight she had spent ages pinning it into what she hoped was a smooth, sophisticated chignon. Her dress was black, and her father would disapprove of that, but it suited her, making her hair look more blonde by contrast, and emphasising smooth skin which had almost lost its summer tan. It had a cape-style frill that formed a sleeve over one arm, but the other shoulder was bare except for a narrow strip of fabric. She would turn up the central heating a little before joining her father to greet their guests.

She put a pair of pearl droplets in her ears, and picked up a perfume spray from the dressing-table. Then she hesitated, opened a drawer and took out a small bottle instead. She unscrewed the stopper and touched the perfume to her inner wrists and elbows, behind her ears and in the hollow at the base of her throat.

She wondered if the Allyn man would recognise it. Her lips curved in a little smile, the mirror catching the image. She leaned closer, and the shoestring strap of her dress slipped down on her shoulder. Adjusting it, she straightened. She felt a strange nervousness about meeting him again. Probably because he had seen that rather embarrassing little incident in the garden at her birthday party, she told herself. He might have shown himself sooner, instead of lurking in the gazebo, watching and listening.

To be fair, he had been in an awkward position. He might have hoped they would go away without seeing him at all.

She frowned at the mirror. Did she look older? A hand went to her hair. Already there were wispy bits trying to escape. Her father's voice penetrated through the door.

'Trista! Our guests are arriving.'

Trista shivered. She crossed to the door and listened for a moment. A woman's voice, and a man's deeper one. Not the Allyn man, then. He had been invited alone, at her father's insistence. 'But he might have a girlfriend,' Trista had said as they discussed who would be invited. 'Even a live-in one.'

'He lives alone,' Geoffrey had told her.

'How do you know?'

'We checked him out pretty thoroughly before inviting him to join the firm,' her father had said. 'A decent, sound young man. What about this Canadian fellow you want to invite? What do you know about him?'

'Not a lot,' Trista had answered. 'That's why I'd like to invite him, to get to know him better. He won't spill the soup or stick his finger in the pudding.'

'Well, don't neglect our other guests, that's all. Pierce doesn't know any of them, remember.'

'Neither does Steve.'

She had met Steve a week ago at a party given by one of her university friends. He was the bronzed, athletic type, who had relations in New Zealand and had been hitch-hiking about the country. Trista had enjoyed talking to him, and on impulse had invited him to the dinner party her father had wanted her to organise for about a dozen people.

As she opened the door, ready to go and greet the first couple to arrive, she hoped that Steve would not be late.

He was there before Pierce Allyn put in his appearance, and she was glad about that. Steve was a relaxing person to be with. When Pierce took her hand in his and said, 'You're wearing the perfume I gave you,' she was able to smile nicely as she replied,

'Perhaps I used too much.'

He shook his head. 'No. It's not too strong. I'm glad you want to use it.'

'This is the first time I've worn it.'

'Oh? In my honour?'

Trista shrugged. 'You could say that. I thought it would be appropriate.'

She introduced him to Steve and the other guests, making small-talk and ensuring that everyone had someone to hold a conversation with, and then excused herself to go and help in the kitchen. Mrs Kemp, the housekeeper, was almost ready to serve the first course. Trista said, 'Five minutes, then, Mrs Kemp. I'll try and get them to finish their drinks and move to the dining-room.'

She accomplished it quite smoothly, and helped to carry in the food before she seated herself. She had placed Steve on her right and made sure the Allyn man was where she didn't have to talk to him during dinner.

Afterwards they went back to the big sitting-room, and she helped the housekeeper to distribute coffee and mints.

Her father was talking to Pierce Allyn. 'Thank you, dear,' he said, taking a mint. 'Didn't I tell you, Pierce, she's a great little hostess when she puts her mind to it?'

'You did indeed,' Pierce answered. She looked up sharply as she presented the mints to him, because his voice held a slight tremor of laughter. 'In fact, I can see,' he added, 'that she's on her best behaviour.'

She was, but as his gaze swept up to her hair she felt suddenly like a little girl dressed up in her mother's clothes. At least, that was the way she thought he saw her.

His eyes returned to hers, and he smiled. She wanted to snap, What's so funny? But that would spoil the image. He took a mint from the dish and said, 'The dinner was superb, thank you. I enjoyed every mouthful.'

'I'll tell Mrs Kemp.'

'Do you cook?' he asked.

'I can.'

'Of course she can,' Geoffrey insisted. 'She's quite a good cook.'

'Thank you for the testimonial, Dad,' she said, 'but I'm not in Mrs Kemp's class, and you know it.'

She moved on, and was thankful when her hostess duties were virtually over and she could sink on to a sofa beside Steve. She wasn't prepared for Pierce to join them, which he did after a short while, sitting on a chair nearby and pleasantly engaging Steve in a discussion about his travels and life in Canada.

She was aware that they both tried to include her too, but although she was scrupulously courteous she found herself competing for Steve's attention. It wasn't difficult. She leaned close as she took his empty cup and offered to get him another, looked at him in a certain way, put a hand on his shoulder as she stood up and, when she returned, sat nearer to him, her thigh touching his.

She heard him falter in mid-sentence, and smiled quietly to herself, casually placing her hand over his where it rested on his knee, her thumb stroking the back of it.

Steve totally lost the thread of the conversation. He turned a bemused face to her, and she gave him a dazzling, intimate smile.

Pierce finished his coffee and said, 'Trista, I wonder if you'd do the same for me?'

She looked at him, the smile faded abruptly, and he smiled in turn, holding out his cup. 'Get me some more coffee?'

When she came back with it, he had moved, and was talking

to her father, standing with him in front of one of the windows. She had to walk the length of the room to take him his cup, and he scarcely paused in what he was saying to take it. 'Thank you, Trista,' he said, glancing at her, and turned back to her father.

Furious, she returned to Steve on the sofa, and he lifted his arm to rest it behind her, but she hardly heard what he said to her. Her eyes were fixed on Pierce Allyn. As though feeling the angry intensity of her gaze, he looked over at her suddenly, and his brows went up in amused enquiry.

Steve said, 'Hey, what's the matter?'

'Nothing. Have you been up to the Waitakeres, Steve?'

'That's those hills near the city? No, but I've been told the views are real nice up there.'

'I'll take you tomorrow, if you like. We could have a picnic. There are beaches, too.'

His hand moved to her shoulder, sliding down her arm.

'Mrs Bridgeman is sitting alone over there,' Trista said, getting up. 'I'd better go and talk to her.'

When the guests started to leave, Pierce was among the first. Geoffrey called his daughter over to say goodnight to him, and she gave him a cool hand and thanked him for coming, without meeting his eyes.

'Thank you for inviting me,' he said. 'It's been an entertaining evening.'

She looked at him then with suspicion, sure there was a gleam of laughter lurking in the grey eyes.

'I'm glad you enjoyed yourself,' she told him rather shortly, and not entirely truthfully.

'Steve seems to be having a good time,' he said, looking at the Canadian. 'In New Zealand,' he added, as though it were an afterthought.

'Yes,' she said. 'We're going to picnic together tomorrow in the Waitakeres.'

'That'll be an experience for him,' Pierce said. 'Although

it could be risky.'

'Risky?'

Geoffrey said, 'People have got lost in the Waitakeres.'

'Steve will be safe with me.' Trista was looking at Pierce.

'I wouldn't count on it,' said Pierce, his tone dry.

Geoffrey laughed. 'Careful there, Pierce. Trista can be quite an ardent feminist about some things.'

'Why should you worry about Steve?' Trista asked Pierce.

'He seems a nice bloke. And he's a visitor to our country.'

'He's a big boy,' she said. 'I think he can be trusted to look after himself.'

Pierce nodded sceptically. 'Well, enjoy yourselves,' he said. 'Goodnight, and thanks again. Both of you.'

The day started well enough. Trista had her own Japanese car, given to her by her father on her eighteenth birthday. She picked up Steve and in less than an hour they were standing on a lookout point, looking across a vista of bush to the city in the distance. Later she drove down one of the winding roads to a beach where they paddled, not quite game to swim although the weather was balmy, and then picnicked on leftovers from dinner the night before and a pie that Trista had baked that morning. Steve stripped off his shirt, and Trista discarded the blouse she wore with a pair of shorts, to reveal a brief top. When Steve made the move she had been expecting, she let him take her in his arms and kiss her, and trailed her fingers across his shoulders, allowing him to press her back on the soft sand. But when his kiss became more passionate she pushed him away and sat up.

'Want to find somewhere more private?' he asked.

'No.' She looked about for her blouse and pulled it on.

'Something wrong?'

'I said a drive and a picnic,' she told him. 'Nothing else.'

'OK,' Steve said equably, but with a note of puzzlement in his voice. 'Sorry if I was out of line. I thought——'

'I know what you thought.'

Steve spread his hands rather helplessly. 'I guess I got a crossed signal. Maybe the girls here are different from back home . . .'

She looked up at him, about to say something cutting, and was hit by a surge of compunction. 'No, they're not,' she said. 'They're not all like me, Steve. Most of them are—nice.'

'*You're* nice.'

Trista shook her head. 'No. It wasn't your fault. I—changed my mind.'

He shrugged. 'Lady's privilege. I'm glad I got to kiss you, though.'

'I don't suppose you've any shortage of girls to kiss,' she said, eyeing his tanned physique.

He grinned. 'Maybe I'm choosy. And maybe you are, too.'

A faintly mocking smile curled her lips. 'Don't jump to conclusions. I'm not so choosy.'

He looked at her quite seriously. 'But you change your mind,' he said. 'Often?'

She was sitting with her knees hunched. She ran a hand up her nape to her hair, bending her head. 'Too often. Someone the other night practically called me a man-eater.'

'What, a little thing like you?' he scoffed. 'I don't believe it.'

She looked round at him, her eyes smiling. 'He thought you might need rescuing.'

Steve laughed. 'From you?'

Trista nodded.

'He's got a nerve, hasn't he? Who was it? The lawyer with the eagle eyes?'

'Do eagles have grey eyes?'

'No, I don't think so. But he didn't miss much last night. It was him, wasn't it?'

'Yes, it was him.'

'Is he interested in you?'

'No.' Trista shook her head. 'I made a pass at him and he slapped me down.'

'*What?*'

'Oh, not literally,' Trista assured him. 'He looked down his nose at me and said he had to be going. One day he'll be a judge. He's got the manner down pat already.'

'*You're* interested in *him*, aren't you?'

'That stuffed shirt?' Trista laughed. 'No, I just thought it would be fun to see how he reacted. I was sure he'd be flustered.'

'And was he?'

'No. Not a bit. So it wasn't much fun after all. Look, forget about him. What do you want to do now? More sightseeing or laze around for a few hours?'

'Let's laze around. Trista—can I see you again before I leave?'

'Are you sure you want to?'

'Of course I'm sure. We're friends, right?'

Trista smiled. 'Just friends?'

'Whenever you want to change that, say the word.'

'No.' Trista said decisively. 'You'll be gone in two weeks, anyway. Friends. I'd like that.'

'Good.' He kissed her cheek lightly. 'Thanks, Triss.'

She didn't see Pierce Allyn again until after Steve had left the country. For two weeks they had spent most of their time together. Steve was on holiday and Trista, was waiting for replies to some job applications. It was two weeks of relaxed enjoyment such as she had seldom experienced before, and the only cloud on the horizon was her father's blatant disapproval.

'I don't see what you've got against Steve,' Trista protested. 'Mrs Bridgeman said he was "wholesome" —don't you think he's wholesome?'

'Sounds like that bread with bits of chaff and seed in it that stick between your teeth,' her father growled. 'He's a glorified hobo, as far as I can see. He told me he's got no job in Canada.'

'I've got no job here,' Trista pointed out.

'You're a girl,' Geoffrey said, as though it made all the difference. 'Anyway, you're at least looking for one.'

'Well, so will Steve be, when he gets back home. He's leaving soon.'

Her father looked at her thoughtfully. 'You'll miss him?'

'Yes, I will. A lot.'

Geoffrey frowned. 'Are you telling me you're serious about this boy?'

Trista smiled. 'You know I'm never serious about men.'

Her father's frown deepened. 'You can't go on forever playing the field. It's time you were thinking about marriage. But not with a Canadian hitch-hiker.'

Trista's eyes narrowed. 'Well, do you have someone in mind?' she asked sweetly.

He opened his mouth, and quickly shut it again. Then he muttered vaguely, 'There are plenty of decent young men about, and you're a pretty enough girl. One day you'll meet someone.'

But she didn't think it was coincidence that the night after Steve left her father invited Pierce over after work, saying they had a case to discuss.

She met them at the door and announced that she was going out for the evening. 'I know you won't mind,' she said, 'as you're working.'

'Of course not,' Pierce said. 'Have a good time.'

'Where are you going?' her father demanded.

'A film. And maybe we'll have supper afterwards.'

'We?'

'Just a few friends.'

'Well, don't be late.'

'Dad, I'm twenty-one.'

'You're still living in my house,' Geoffrey reminded her. 'Don't be late.'

She was late, more so because her car broke down, and she left it on the side of the road a few blocks from the house and started walking home.

When a car going in the opposite direction slowed and stopped just ahead of her, she kept walking briskly but moved to the inner side of the footpath.

As she passed it, the shadowy figure in the driver's seat leaned across to open the passenger door. Trista quickened her pace.

'Trista!'

She stopped and turned. Pierce opened the driver's door and got out, coming towards her. 'I thought you had a car.'

'I do. It broke down.'

'Hop in. I'll take you home.'

'It's all right. It's only a short way.'

'Your father wouldn't like——'

'Oh, *damn* what my father wouldn't like!'

There was a short silence. Then Pierce said mildly, 'Come on. There's no sense in courting danger.' He took her arm, and after a second she stopped pulling stiffly against his hold and allowed him to put her into the car.

'It's actually quite safe around here,' she said, as he started the engine again.

'You can't be sure of being safe anywhere,' he argued.

'You lawyers are all alike,' she said. 'The job warps your view of human nature.'

Surprisingly, he laughed. 'You could be right.'

'Anyway,' she said, 'I gather that you consider me a danger to mankind, rather than the other way about.'

'Did I give you that impression?'

'Don't hedge. You know you did.'

'Why are you so angry?'

'Oh, come on, Mr Allyn. You know all about scorned women, don't you?'

'Are you a woman scorned, then?' He cast her an unreadable look.

'Aren't I?' she said lightly. 'You certainly made it clear that you weren't interested.'

'Well, I've always felt rather sorry for mice,' he explained.

She turned in the seat to look at him. 'You're hardly a mouse. Is that what you were trying to prove?'

'I wasn't trying to prove anything. What were *you* trying to prove?'

'Wasn't it obvious?' she challenged him.

His glance was appreciative. 'Yes. As a matter of fact it was. You felt I'd seen you at a disadvantage, and you wanted to wind me round your little finger to get your own back.'

'You must be a demon in court.'

'I get by. It would probably have worked with a younger man. You were out of your league, that's all.'

'Don't patronise me!' she snapped.

'Sorry.' He drew up in front of her house. 'It's just a bit difficult to treat an adolescent *femme fatale* like a mature woman.'

Her breath hissed between her teeth. Delivered in a cool, considering tone, the remark had been deliberate and calculated.

'As difficult as believing that a pompous, cold-blooded barrister with an inflated ego could be hiding a real man inside the image?' she demanded, adding with the utmost contempt, 'You probably can't even kiss a girl without cross-examining her first, and passing judgement afterwards.

She threw open the door of the car and slammed it behind her. But before she reached the house he caught her up on the pathway. His hand grasped hers and swung her round. 'If you wanted to be kissed that badly, Trista,' he said, 'all you had to do was ask me nicely.'

The next second she was in his arms, her hands trapped between them, and his mouth was on hers, warm and firm.

He made a thorough job of it, very confident and very expert. He took it slowly at first, but, when her lips parted under the insistent pressure of his, he pulled her closer and took her mouth deeply, until she gave a surprised little moan and tried to push away.

He let her go without haste, holding her a foot away with his hands on her arms. 'There,' he said, on a note of satisfaction.

And then he was striding across the footpath to the car without a backward glance.

CHAPTER THREE

NONE of Trista's job applications bore fruit. Her Arts degree apparently overqualified her for some positions, and was regarded as insufficient on its own for others. Some of her friends had moved away and others had entered the workforce. 'I'm beginning to feel like a parasite on society,' she told one of them, and tried for a place on a computer-programming and keyboard-skills course at a business college. 'I may as well learn something useful, if no one will employ me,' she told her father, asking him for the money to pay the term fees.

'I suppose so,' he agreed. 'Are you sure you wouldn't like to go into teaching?'

'I'm sure.' She could think of nothing worse than spending her days with a roomful of other people's children. 'And before you mention nursing, it's no again. We've had this discussion before.'

'The Legal Society's Annual Ball is on in three weeks,' Geoffrey said. 'I hope you'll come with me.'

Trista moved restlessly. 'Do you really think that's necessary.'

'I would like you to come,' Geoffrey repeated. 'Is it too much to ask? I don't often make a request like this, Trista.'

'If it's so important to you, all right, I'll come.'

Her father relaxed. 'Good. Buy yourself a pretty dress. Something special. I'll pay for it. That should sweeten the pill.'

'You think you can bribe me into anything, don't you?'

'It's not a bribe, it's a present. Can't you accept it in the spirit that it's offered?'

'Sorry. I'm not much of a daughter to you, am I?'

'You're a very lovely girl, and clever, too. If you've been a bit—silly at times, well, all young people make mistakes. It takes time to mature. It's a pity about your mother . . . I know we don't always manage to see eye to eye, my dear, but believe me, I've done my best.'

'Yes. Yes, I know.' She hesitated. 'Do you ever have doubts about what's best? Have you ever been sorry——'

'No use crying over spilt milk,' Geoffrey said briskly. 'It does no good to dwell on the past, Trista. I learned that when your mother died. Pick up and go on, that's the only way. If we spent our lives wondering if we'd done the right thing, made the right choices about problems in the past, we'd never get anything done in the future, and the future is what counts. You've got your whole life ahead of you. All I want is for you to be happy. It's all I ever wanted for you.'

She believed that. But her father had always been so certain that he knew what would make her happy . . . And he hadn't changed. She realised that when she went to the ball, in a new chiffon dress with a swirling skirt and strapless bodice, and found that Pierce Allyn was one of the party at her father's table, and that he had come without a partner. At her father's suggestion, she had no doubt.

When he asked her to dance she got up reluctantly, but he was so good at it that soon she began to relax and enjoy herself.

'Don't you have a girlfriend you could have brought along tonight?' she asked him.

'None I particularly wanted to bring,' he answered. 'What's happened to Steve?'

'He went back to Canada.' She glanced up at him and added, 'Unscathed.'

Pierce smiled slightly. 'Are you sure?'

'Yes.'

'And what about you?'

'What?' She looked up at him, puzzled.

'Are *you* unscathed?'

'Me?' Trista raised her brows. 'Of course. I don't let men——'

'Hurt you?' he suggested, after a moment. His gaze was uncomfortably searching. 'What are you frightened of, Trista?'

'Frightened?' She gave him a scornful look. 'What on earth gives you that idea? You're off on the wrong scent entirely.'

'Am I?' he said sceptically.

'An amateur psychologist, are you?' she scoffed. 'You know what they say about a little knowledge.'

'It's a dangerous thing. Yes, I know. Perhaps you should remember it, too.'

'What do you mean?'

'That was a fairly dangerous situation you got yourself into at your birthday party. If you make a habit of goading impressionable young men, you can expect to find yourself out of your depth one day.'

In a cold little voice, she said, 'I don't know what you think gives you the right to criticise me—I get enough of that from my father.'

'I wasn't criticising you. I was warning you. Out of—concern for your welfare, if you like.'

'That's what he always says. It's for my own good. But you're not my father—and you know nothing about me——'

'I do know something about men,' Pierce said. 'And how they're likely to react to the kind of treatment you dish out. I've seen the results in court, and believe me, they're not pretty.'

'As you saw, I can look after myself.'

'In your father's home, with plenty of people about, maybe. In a different situation, you might not have found an aggressive male so easy to deal with.'

'Men,' Trista said, 'are always easy to deal with.' Her tone was bored, but her eyes lifted to challenge him. As she met the grey gaze, her heart skipped a beat. He looked as though he wanted to shake her, and she felt his hand tighten on hers.

Quite softly, he said, 'I don't believe you know the first thing about *men*, Trista. You've been playing around with boys until now.' She could see the unspoken thought in his eyes. It's time you learned: time somebody taught you a lesson.

Trista felt a surge of adrenalin through her veins, a premonition of excitement. Pierce's eyes narrowed, a grim little smile touching his mouth.

The music stopped and he guided her back to the table. Then he excused himself to go and talk to some people in another group, and she saw him take one of the woman on to the dance-floor. There was something about formal evening clothes on a man, she thought. They made Pierce look remarkably handsome.

His partner, a tall, slim, red-headed girl, was talking to him, and he seemed to be giving her all his attention, but once he glanced up and caught Trista's eye, and his mouth quirked in a tiny, somehow intimate smile. Trista turned away to engage in a lively conversation with one of the other men at the table.

Pierce rejoined the party, and they danced together several times. At the end of one bracket, as the music became slow and romantic, and the lights dim, he tightened his hold and drew her to him.

Trista stiffened and pushed at his chest.

'What's the matter?' he asked.

'I don't like dancing like this.'

'Liar. Put your arms around me.'

'No.' She stopped moving, her body quite rigid, and he smiled down into her defiant eyes and said, 'All right, Mary, Mary.' His lips brushed her forehead, and then he released her. His hand on her waist, he said, 'We'll go back to the table.'

When they reached it, her father said, 'Trista, I'm a little tired. I think I'll go home.'

'All right,' she said, picking up the small silver bag she had brought with her.

'No, no!' Geoffrey said. 'No need for you to come. Pierce won't mind getting you a taxi later, will you, Pierce?'

'I'll bring her home myself,' Pierce promised, as she was sure her father had expected.

'I'll come with you,' she insisted. But Geoffrey wouldn't hear of it, and Pierce put a hand on her wrist and said, 'Leave it. I'll take you home as soon as you like. Your father doesn't want to spoil your evening.'

When Geoffrey had gone, and the other couples had all left the table for the dance-floor or the bar, she sat fiddling with the bag in her hands. 'I'm sorry,' she said.

'Sorry? For what?'

Impatiently, she looked up. 'You must realise by now what my father is trying to do.'

'Throw us together? Yes, of course I do. I'm flattered.'

'Flattered?'

'That he thinks me good enough for his daughter.'

'Don't you mind? Being manipulated, I mean.'

'Do you?'

'Yes.' She put the bag down on the table with a small thud. 'Why do you go along with it? Because he's your boss?'

Pierce said, 'There are other reasons. Which must have occurred to you.'

She lifted her eyes to his face. 'You don't *like* me.'

His smile was a little crooked. 'Liking doesn't necessarily have a lot to do with it. I'd have thought you'd have found out that much by now.'

A strange feeling of grief constricted her chest, and she turned her head away.

His hand come out to cover hers where it lay on the table.

'What's the matter?' he said.

She looked down at the strong fingers enclosing hers, and then smiled at him. 'Nothing. Whatever made you ask that?'

His eyes had that narrowed look again, and she moved uneasily. 'Let's dance,' she suggested, sliding her hand away from his clasp and pushing back her chair.

He didn't hold her close this time and they talked little. She tried to join in the conversation at the table afterwards, but was increasingly conscious of Pierce sitting at her side, his arm casually resting on the back of her chair. When she leaned back, she felt the brush of his sleeve against her skin.

When the compère announced the end of the evening, she said, 'Get me a taxi, please, Pierce.'

'No.' He handed her bag to her and took her arm. 'Come on.'

As they reached the car park, she said, 'It's out of your way.'

He glanced down at her without speaking, his hand urging her towards his car. As he unlocked the door for her, she shivered. He straightened and ran a hand down her arm. 'Don't you have a wrap or something?'

'I left it in Dad's car.'

'Here,' he said, taking off his jacket.

'There's no need——'

He placed it round her shoulders and put her into the passenger seat. The silk lining of the jacket was warm from his body. As he slid in beside her, she said, 'Aren't you cold?'

'I'm wearing a long-sleeved shirt,' he pointed out. 'That dress is hardly practical for this time of year, is it?'

'I wasn't cold inside. It's a very expensive dress.'

He gave a slight laugh, and started the engine. 'Do you want to go straight home?'

'Yes.'

His driving was competent and careful, and he stayed within the speed limit. When they stopped at her gate, she said, 'Thank you for bringing me home.'

'No trouble.' He got out and came round to help her out. She slipped off his jacket. 'And thanks for this.'

Taking it from her, Pierce said, 'Like to come out with me tomorrow?'

'No, I—don't think so.'

'Chicken,' he jeered softly.

Trista gave a tiny shrug. 'If you like to think so.'

'You're tired,' he said. 'Call me if you change your mind.'

He started to turn away, and she said, 'I won't call.'

He swung back to her. 'OK, I'll call *you*. About ten. Or is that too early for you on a Sunday?'

'I don't want to go out with you.'

'Don't you?' He lifted her chin as he had once before, and she stood quite still as he touched her lips with his. 'I'll ask you again tomorrow.'

He got back into the car, and she muttered, 'And I'll say no again tomorrow.'

But somehow she didn't. They had lunch at a city restaurant and spent the afternoon at the art gallery, viewing an exhibition of contemporary prints. His manner was relaxed and urbane, and she found herself responding to it, becoming less tense and more spontaneous.

He said hello to several people who were there, and introduced her to a man and woman in their late twenties, Calum and Glenda McGregor. 'They're both doctors,' he told her, 'in practice together.'

They looked at Trista with friendly interest. 'What do you do for a living, Trista?' Glenda asked.

Trista grimaced. 'I don't. At the moment I'm unemployed, but I've been taking a business course that I hope will help me get a job.'

'I'm sure it will.' Glenda smiled at her warmly, and Pierce said,

'Trista got her BA just last year.'

They stood chatting for a while, and Pierce said, 'Why don't we all have some coffee together somewhere?'

Calum looked at his watch. 'Sorry, we've got a babysitter, and we're due home in less than half an hour.'

'I've a better idea,' Glenda said. 'Why don't you two come round to our place, and stay for dinner?'

Pierce looked at Trista. 'OK?' he asked. 'If it's not too much trouble for you, Glenda.'

'I wouldn't have asked you if it was.'

Trista said, 'Thank you. I'd like to come.'

'Give us time to make the place presentable,' Calum suggested. 'See you soon, then?'

'They seem nice,' Trista said, as they hurried off.

'They are. Glenda and I used to flat together in my university days—with some others,' he added, seeing her quick glance of enquiry.

The McGregors lived in a pleasant, roomy old house in a tree-lined avenue in the established suburb of Meadowbank. Calum met them, wearing a towel round his waist and with water splashes down the front of his shirt. 'It's bath time,' he explained. 'Glenda's trying to get a nappy on Jennifer—that's what the screaming's about, she's not murdering the child—and I'm dealing with David.' Raising his voice slightly over the indignant crying in the background, he added, 'You know where the drinks are, Pierce. Get one for yourself and Trista.' And he disappeared back to the bathroom.

Glenda came into the lounge a few minutes later as Pierce handed Trista a glass. She had a pyjama-clad infant in her arms, curly-haired and with tears on its fat cheeks, but now beaming toothlessly.

'Sorry about that,' she said. 'Pierce, be a love and pour me a sherry, please. I can do with it.'

She sat down and Pierce gave her a drink, which she deftly held out of the baby's small, seeking hands, turning her head to take sips from it.

She put down the drink on a side table and placed the baby on the floor, but immediately it wailed, blue eyes filling with tears. 'Oh, all right, Jenny-wren,' her mother sighed, picking her up again. 'You're hungry, aren't you? Well, we'll do something about that just as soon as I've had my drink.'

The baby hiccuped and quieted, gazing round the room and finding the visitors with a look composed of interest and suspicion. Glenda finished her sherry and stood up. 'Come on, then, my beautiful,' she said. 'Excuse me, you two. I'll just see what I can do about filling this bottomless pit here.' She tickled her daughter's tummy, and the baby chortled as Glenda carried her from the room.

Calum brought in a little boy wrapped in a towel. He talked to Pierce and Trista while he dried the child, who kept turning to stare at the visitors, and put a pair of pyjamas on its wriggling limbs. Then he said, 'Say goodnight, son, and hop into bed.'

'Hungry,' David announced firmly.

'You've been fed.'

'Hungry,' the boy repeated plaintively.

'All right, go in the kitchen and ask your mother for a bit of cheese or something.'

Calum poured himself a drink, which he was half-way through when David appeared again in the doorway. 'Bed, Daddy.'

'Thank heaven!' Calum exclaimed, putting down his glass. 'One down, one to go.' He picked up his son, swinging him to his shoulder. 'Say goodnight to the visitors.'

David waved to them. 'Goo'night.'

'Goodnight, David,' Trista and Pierce answered.

'Be back with you in a couple of minutes,' his father assured them. 'And you *will* get dinner. Glenda's got it underway.'

When they had gone, Trista said hesitantly, 'Do you think Glenda would like some hlep?'

'Ask her,' Pierce suggested.

Trista got up, but as she went towards the door Glenda appeared with Jennifer cradled in one arm, and a bottle in the other hand.

Trista stepped back. 'I was coming to see if you could do with a hand.'

'Well, you could give this to her,' Glenda said gratefully. 'Then I can get on with the dinner—mind, it's only going to be tinned soup, and cold meat with salad and microwaved potatoes.'

Trista automatically took the bottle from Glenda's outstretched hand, but when Glenda made to hand her the baby, she took a step back, her face tight with panic. 'I don't know anything about babies. I'm sorry.'

Glenda laughed. 'Don't worry, there's nothing to it. Sit down first—you can't drop her then. I'll show you how to hold her.'

For a moment Trista remained standing, casting a glance at Pierce that plainly said, *Help*!

He was looking at her quizzically, obviously with no intention of coming to the rescue, and she subsided into a chair, allowing Glenda to arrange the baby in her arms.

'Just keep the bottle up so she isn't swallowing air,' Glenda said.

'Yes, all right,' Trista said in strangled tones. 'You—you won't be long, will you? I won't know what to do if she cries.'

'Most unlikely with a full tummy. And she hardly ever spits, either. Not like David. He was a horrible baby, forever throwing his milk up.'

She left them, and Trista, after watching baby and bottle carefully for a minute, and realising that Jennifer knew what she was about, even if her temporary nursemaid didn't, looked up to see an expression of unholy enjoyment on Pierce's face.

'What's so funny?' she hissed at him, afraid of disturbing the baby's concentration.

He laughed aloud. 'You holding a baby. It somehow doesn't

seem quite right.'

A searing anger shook her, her eyes blazing before she looked away from him, her face shuttered, as the anger was replaced by something else.

Pierce stopped laughing. 'Hey!' he said, crossing over to her, and sitting on the arm of the chair, his hand on her shoulder. 'I'm sorry.'

She kept her eyes on the baby, who was staring up at her with a wide blue gaze. 'It doesn't matter,' she said, her voice muffled with the effort of keeping it low. 'And take your hand off me!'

He removed it to the back of the chair, but he was still too close.

'You think you're so clever,' she said. 'Don't you ever look under the surface of a person?'

Why had she said that? It was inviting him to probe, the last thing she wanted.

The baby pushed the teat out of its mouth, and when Trista tried to replace it, turned away with a grimace.

'I think she's telling you she's had enough,' Pierce said, standing up. 'Shouldn't you pat her back or something?'

'How should I know?' Trista placed the bottle on the side table with her own glass. 'You've just told me I'm incompetent.'

He said, 'That's not what I said at all. Just that the Madonna look doesn't agree with the image you like to present to the world.' His glance fell to the baby. 'Anyway, she seems quite happy.'

Jennifer was smiling beatifically, her hands waving as she looked at Trista's face. Instinctively Trista gave her a finger to hold, and returned the smile, gazing back. She hoped that Pierce couldn't see the expression on her face. There was a strange melting sensation inside her as she bent over the tiny body that fitted so snugly into the crook of her arm, and Jennifer's fingers curled warmly about the one she held out for her. 'Hello, Jennifer,' she said softly. 'I'm Trista. And you're a beautiful little girl, aren't you?'

Jennifer cooed and wriggled with delight. Trista went on talking to her, and when Glenda came back into the room Pierce was still standing in the middle of it, watching them both.

'Right, all under control,' Glenda announced. 'How did it go, Trista?'

'She didn't finish her bottle,' Trista said.

'Naughty girl.' Glenda stooped to take her daughter, and Trista relinquished her reluctantly. 'Too interested in a new face, eh?'

Glenda held the baby under the arms, level with her own laughing face. Jennifer giggled. 'Yes, I know,' Glenda told her with mock sternness. 'And you'll be asking for more in the middle of the night. Now come on, and no more nonsense, my girl!'

She picked up the bottle and sat down, and this time the baby emptied it before turning to grin at Trista.

'She's taken a fancy to you,' Glenda announced.

'I've taken a fancy to her, too. She's gorgeous.'

Calum returned then. 'We think so,' he said, 'but then we're biased, aren't we?' He grinned at his wife. 'David's all tucked up. I read him the shortest story on record.'

'You're next,' Glenda informed her daughter. 'Come on, my lovely, bedtime for little girls.'

'Could I come?' Trista asked.

'Yes, of course.'

The baby objected with a little whimper as Glenda lowered her into the cot, but when a stuffed rabbit was tucked in beside her under the blankets she seemed ready to settle down, even though her eyes were wide open.

'Goodnight, honeybunch,' her mother said firmly, and kissed her.

'Could I give her a kiss?' Trista asked impulsively, as

Glenda made to slide up the side of the cot.

'Yes, sure.' Glenda stepped back, and Trista put her lips to a rose-petal cheek. 'Goodnight, darling,' she whispered.

As she straightened, she touched her own cheek, brushing back a wisp of hair.

Glenda secured the cot and turned out the light. Reluctantly Trista left the baby and followed her hostess to the door. 'You are lucky,' she said.

'Yes, I know. Mind you, this is the best time of the day, when they're bathed and fed and into bed,' she added as they headed for the kitchen. 'They're at their sweetest then. It's not so hot when they're crawling about the floor getting in the way and shoving any revolting object they find into their mouths and slobbering over everything. Not to mention the nappies, of course. Not my favourite part of motherhood. Do go back to the lounge if you'd like, Trista. Have another drink while you're waiting.'

'If I'm not in the way,' Trista said diffidently. 'I'd rather stay and help.'

'Bless you, love, I'd be delighted.'

When they were all seated at the table, Glenda said, 'I believe we've made poor Trista quite clucky. I've tried to tell her about the less pleasant aspects of parenthood, but she keeps asking questions like, "When will Jennifer be crawling?" and "How soon do they talk?" She even wants to know if it's bad for a baby not to be breast-fed for the first few months. I'm afraid she's a hopeless case.'

Trista coloured, and Glenda added quickly, 'Oh, I'm *sorry*, love.' She leaned over to pat Trista's hand. 'Being a doctor, *and* a mother, I tend to come out with these things. I was forgetting how young you are.'

Trista accepted the apology with a smile, but she noticed the quick, rueful look that Calum shot Pierce. 'You must find it tiring,' she said to Glenda, 'managing a career and a young family.'

'We share both,' Glenda explained, looking at her husband. 'It is a strain sometimes, but I wouldn't want it any other way. I couldn't bear to give up my work, and Calum likes spending time with the kids.'

'Yes,' Calum agreed. 'Although I could strangle young David when he decides to get stroppy. But then, I have patients who bring out homicidal tendencies in me, too.'

'I think I'd want to be a full-time mother,' Trista said. Then, flushing again, she added hastily, 'That wasn't a criticism.'

'I didn't think it was,' Glenda assured her. 'Everyone is different. Fortunately the times are long gone when a woman who wanted a career had to give up the thought of a family. Now you can have both, not easily, but with a lot of organisation and the right husband. All the same, sometimes I envy women who are happy with one career—whether it's a professional one or the traditional career of home and bringing up children. And if that's what a woman—or a man, for that matter—wants to do, I believe she or he should be allowed to do it. And not be put down by people who don't seem to realise how much intelligence and patience and sheer hard work that takes.'

'Yes, my love,' Calum said affectionately. 'Shall I help you down off your soap-box now?'

Glenda grimaced at him, and Trista was fascinated to see the resemblance to Jennifer's repudiation of her bottle.

Pierce said suddenly, 'Shouldn't you have let your father know you wouldn't be home until after dinner, Trista?'

'It's all right,' she said. 'I'm sure he won't worry while he knows I'm with you.'

The mention of her father changed her mood, and the look he gave her told her that he had caught the faint sarcasm in her tone.

Calum said, 'Use our phone, if you like.'

'Thank you, but I'm over twenty-one, and there's no need, honestly.'

'Enjoyed yourself?' Pierce asked her on their way home.

'Very much. They're an interesting couple, aren't they?'

Pierce agreed, then laughed quietly. 'I think they find us an interesting couple, too.'

'You mean, they wonder what you see in me?'

'Don't be touchy,' he chided. 'That isn't exactly difficult to fathom.' He cast her a sideways glance that made her instantly, annoyingly breathless.

'Is that supposed to be a compliment?' she asked tartly.

'What should I say?' he asked her. 'That I'm attracted to your mind?'

'I don't think you're attracted at all. Not really.'

His brows went up, and he turned to her again before giving his attention to the road. 'Then why do you suppose I asked you to come with me today?'

She looked at him consideringly. 'Because of my father.'

'You think he suggested it?'

'Not exactly. But I think you'd—like to please him. He can do your career a lot of good, can't he?'

'Yes,' Pierce kept his eyes on the road, his voice level.

'Well, at least you're honest.'

He smiled faintly. 'It does help that you look the way you do. And,' he added deliberately, 'kiss the way you do.'

'I've had lots of practice,' she admitted. And was gratified to see the smile disappear. She sat looking at his impassive face for a minute or so, then gazed out at the darkened street, a faint smile curving her own lips.

CHAPTER FOUR

PIERCE walked her to the door, and drew her into his arms. Trista didn't object, lifting her face for his kiss, the smile still on her lips. For a few seconds he stared down at her, and she thought that he had changed his mind. Then he lowered his head and his lips touched her mouth, and a current of excitement rippled over her. Her mouth parted in invitation, but he didn't take advantage of it right away. In fact, she thought he checked for a moment, before his lips began playing over hers, tantalisingly, until with a kind of desperation she wound her arms about his neck and went on tiptoe, silently begging him to end the sweet suspense.

At last he did. His tongue slid into her mouth and she accepted it eagerly, savouring the taste and texture of him, passionately glad when she felt the involuntary tightening of his arms, and heard his breathing quicken.

When at last his hold slackened and he raised his mouth from hers, he said, 'Practice makes perfect.' But his voice was not quite normal, and Trista, her tongue running round slightly bruised lips, felt a stab of triumph.

A light went on behind the glass panels of the door, and the catch rattled.

Trista started almost guiltily, moving away from him, but Pierce kept a firm arm about her waist and turned to face her father as he opened the door.

'Thought I heard something,' Geoffrey said. 'I expected you home hours ago.'

'My fault, I'm afraid,' Pierce said. 'We had dinner with friends of mine, and we didn't think of the time.'

Trista said, 'Actually, Pierce suggested I should phone. It isn't his fault at all.'

'Well, now that you're here,' Geoffrey said, 'come in. Trista will make you some coffee.'

Pierce looked at her rebellious face. 'Thank you very much, but we've had quite a long day. Another time, perhaps.'

He let Trista go then, and left without a backward glance.

'You might have let me know,' Geoffrey told Trista as he closed the door.

'Sorry,' she said. 'I thought you trusted your blue-eyed boy.'

'Of course I trust Pierce. But I didn't know you were going out for dinner.'

'It isn't as though Mrs Kemp had cooked one,' Trista said. Weekends were Mrs Kemp's days off, unless they had guests, and she always left them a cold roast and the makings of a salad. If Trista wanted to cook something she did, but there was plenty to eat if she didn't.

'That's not the point,' Geoffrey argued.

'Is there one?'

'Don't be insolent to me, miss.'

'Look, Dad, I'm not a child any longer. I'm twenty-one and not under your parental control——'

'While you live under my roof you'll have some consideration for my feelings, my girl! Perhaps I don't have the right to ask you where you're going and what you're doing, but it's basic courtesy to let me know if you're going to be late home.'

Trista opened her mouth to retort, then swallowed and said, 'Yes, you're right. I'm sorry, Dad. Next time I will do that.'

Geoffrey nodded. 'Good.'

On her way to her room, she paused and turned. 'But you might as well know, I intend to leave as soon as I get a job and can afford a flat.' She didn't wait for him to reply.

Instead of undressing straight away, she sat with her chin on her hand, gazing into the dressing-table mirror. Her mouth looked red and tender, and she touched it with her fingers and remembered how she had felt when Pierce kissed her.

He was older and more experienced than anyone else she had gone out with. Was that why she found him more exciting? But he hadn't been totally unmoved, either. 'He's a challenge,' she said to her reflection. 'That's what it is. And you're a bitch.'

He knows, her mind said. He knows what you're up to. 'What *am* I up to?' she asked aloud. For the first time in a long while, she wasn't sure.

Playing with fire.

'Maybe. But what about him? Isn't he doing the same? He wasn't so indifferent, tonight. No,' her lips curved, 'not at all indifferent.'

And you?

She saw the flush rise to her cheeks. 'He's good at kissing. Well, he's had plenty of time to learn. He's probably terrific in bed.' The flush spread over her body. She could feel it. She closed her eyes as a shiver of desire followed it.

It's a dangerous game you're playing. Out of your league, he said. Remember?

Opening her eyes, she stared defiantly at her reflection. 'I don't care. I'm bored out of my skull with stupid boys who fall flat at the sight of a pretty face, and get all offended when I let them know I'm not interested any more.'

Yes, you're a bitch, all right. Do you think Pierce would stand for that sort of treatment?

He wouldn't, of course. She shivered again, this time not with desire. 'Don't be silly,' she scolded herself. 'Pierce isn't a brute. He'd probably bow politely and walk out of your life. Forever.'

The thought depressed her, and she shook her head, got

up and started preparing for bed. She wished she had a girlfriend to confide in. Her best friend of childhood had moved to Australia when they were twelve, and gradually their desultory correspondence had lapsed. There had been girls at high school with whom she had exchanged secrets, but not since she was fifteen and had first started dating with boys had she had a close female friend.

Or any close friend, really. She thought of Steve. But this wasn't something she could share with any man. There had been a postcard from him a few days ago. Trista had not replied yet. Probably she never would. Realistically she knew that, although she would value the memory, their relationship was doomed not to last. It had nothing to do, she told the uncomfortable inner voice, with the fact that Steve had been more perceptive than most of the men she knew, and that with him she had briefly let down her guard.

Pierce had made no arrangements to see her again, and after two weeks she was sure that he was not going to. Either that, or he was deliberately keeping her in suspense, hoping she'd jump at the offer when he did ask her to go out with him again. Well, he'd be out of luck, she decided. She was finding the courses at the college tiring, and her social life lately had been somewhat lean. No matter how tempting he made it, she would turn him down.

But when they met again it was by accident. Her aunt had asked her if she would like to accompany her to the theatre. Aunt Hester, her father's sister, was addicted to theatre, and being a widow would buy two tickets and take a friend or her only niece along for company. This time it was Trista's turn. At the interval she got drinks for herself and Hester, and was carefully carrying them back through the crowd to where Hester had found a seat when she saw Pierce, with his arm around the shoulder of a girl, shepherding her through to the bar.

The girl was about her own age, with a peppery

sprinkling of freckles on her nose and a shining fall of shoulder-length brown hair. Trista stood staring, and Pierce looked up and saw her. She flicked her eyes away immediately, and resumed her passage. Apparently he liked them young, she thought. The girl looked fresh and unspoiled, and very pleased with life.

'Well, what do you think of it?' said Hester.

Trista looked at her blankly.

'The play, dear. What do you think of it?'

'Oh, it's very good, isn't it?' She wrenched her mind away from Pierce.

But minutes later his deep voice said, 'Hello, Trista.'

Trista took a gulp of her wine, and fixed a smile to her face before she looked up. 'Pierce! How are you?'

The girl stood beside him, looking at Trista with undisguised curiosity. Well, that's mutual, Trista thought.

'Fine,' Pierce answered. 'You look as beautiful as ever.'

Hester said, 'Good evening. You were at Trista's birthday party.'

'Pierce Allyn,' Trista reminded her. 'This is my aunt, Mrs Wordsworth.'

'I don't think we were formally introduced,' Pierce said, taking the hand Hester extended to him. He turned to the girl at his side. 'This is my sister, Charley.'

'Your sister?' Trista repeated blankly.

He looked at her, his eyes crinkling. 'I told you about her.'

'My name's Charlotte,' the girl said. 'But everyone calls me Charley. Pierce told me about you, too.'

Trista intercepted the quelling glance that Pierce directed at the girl, and naturally felt a consuming desire to know what he had said. Pierce turned to Hester and asked her opinion of the play.

'Well, he mentioned you to the family,' Charley amended. 'What I mean was, I know who you are.'

Trista wondered why she seemed embarrassed. There was more to this, she was sure, than met the eye. She said, 'Are there just the two of you? Pierce told me there was a big age gap between you.'

'Oh, we have another sister, Antonia. She's a year older than Pierce. She's married with two children.'

'Pierce never mentioned her.'

'Have you seen quite a lot of him?' Charley asked with surprise.

'Oh, no! I've met him a few times, that's all.' Obviously Pierce hadn't confided much in his sister, after all. Or perhaps the fact that he had once taken her out wasn't important enough to tell his family about.

The bell rang for the end of the interval and people began hurrying back into the theatre. As Hester stood up, Pierce leaning forward to give her a hand, Charley said, 'Pierce, why don't we all have a late supper after the show?'

If Pierce didn't fancy the idea, he was too well-mannered to show it. Smiling at Hester, he said, 'Would you care to join us?'

'That would be lovely! Thank you.'

'We'll meet you in the lobby, then,' he promised. 'See you later.'

Pierce chose the restaurant and insisted on paying for their supper. Her aunt, Trista realised, was totally charmed. He directed most of his attention to her, and although she enjoyed talking to Charley, who was friendly and forthcoming and occasionally funny, Trista was seething as they walked back to where she had parked her car. Her aunt didn't like driving at night, and if her companion provided the transport she felt that that made up for her buying the tickets.

Trista unlocked the passenger door first, and Pierce opened it for her aunt. By the time he came round to her side, she was fastening her safety-belt. She wound down the

window and said, 'Thank you for the supper. Goodnight,
Charley. It was nice meeting you.'

Pierce put his hand on the doorframe. 'Drive carefully.'

'I'm always careful.' She turned the key and the engine
purred.

Pierce laughed quietly. 'Then you've changed in the last
few weeks.'

Trista started winding up the window, and he removed
his hands and stepped back, giving her a casual wave as the
car moved past him.

'So that's the boss's daughter,' Charley said after they had
got into Pierce's car. Charley was staying at his flat in town
that night, intending to take a bus back home the next day,
Sunday. 'Why is she angry with you?'

Pierce swung the car into the flow of traffic before
answering. 'What makes you think she's angry with me?'

'I just know it—and so do you, I'll bet. What's going on?'

'Nothing is going on. And even if it were, it would be
none of your business, Miss Nosey Parker.'

Undaunted, Charley said, 'I'd like to know what you've
done to her. And don't give me that courtroom look. I'm
your baby sister, and it doesn't work with me.'

Reluctantly, Pierce laughed. 'There was a time when you
were easier to handle.'

'I've grown up. I thought you'd noticed.'

'You still seem very young to me.'

'Does Trista?' she asked curiously.

'Even younger—sometimes.'

Charley cast an interested look at the sudden faint frown
between his brows.

'She's very pretty,' she said.

'Yes. And very much aware of it.'

'She'd be silly if she wasn't aware of it, Pierce. You can't
blame her for that.'

'There are plenty of pretty girls in the world. They don't all use their looks as a weapon.'

'*Does* she?' Pierce didn't answer. After a moment, Charley said, 'Perhaps it's the only weapon she has.'

Pierce gave her a sharp glance. 'Sometimes you surprise me. Why are you defending her?'

'Well—I quite liked her, and besides . . .'

'Besides . . . what?' Pierce prompted.

'I don't really know why, but I was sort of sorry for her.'

'*Sorry* for her?'

'Yes. There's something . . . as though someone's hurt her.'

Pierce said positively, 'It wasn't me.' He looked at his sister with a new respect, recalling his first meeting with Trista, and that odd instinct to comfort.

'Are you sure?'

At Charley's sceptical expression, he said with a hint of impatience, 'Look, I hardly know the girl. But she's definitely not an object of pity. She's the adored daughter of a very well-off father, she's exceptionally good-looking, has plenty of friends, a very adequate social life, I'm certain, and as many men at her feet as any woman could want.'

'Maybe none of them is the man she really wants.'

With considerable feeling, Pierce said, 'How I pity *him*!'

'Why?' Charley asked curiously.

'Because she'll have him for breakfast—and I don't mean in a romantic sense.'

'Are you *frightened* of her?' Charley asked, astonished.

'Don't be silly!' Pierce answered in his most crushing tone. 'Trista Vandeleur is nothing but a mixed-up kid with a nasty habit of chewing up young men and spitting them out. I don't find that especially attractive, but she certainly doesn't *frighten* me! I just don't particularly fancy being next on the menu.'

'Did she want you to be?'

Pierce lifted a shoulder. 'There were signs.'

'But you weren't tempted?'

A crease appeared in his cheek, close by his mouth. 'Any man would be tempted.'

'So?'

'So nothing.'

Charley eyed him suspiciously. Pierce gave an exasperated, slightly embarrassed little laugh. 'She's only a few months older than you,' he pointed out.

'What's that got to do with anything?'

Pierce groaned. 'Leave it, Charley!' he pleaded.

Instead, she turned in the seat, resting her arm on the back of it, and stared at him. 'You *are* tempted!' she said on a note of triumph.

'I told you I was.'

'So why bring her age into it? It seems totally irrelevant to me.'

As the car entered the cul-de-sac where he lived, he said, 'All right. She challenged me, and I succumbed temporarily to a rather self-righteous desire to teach her a lesson. Then I realised how young she was, and decided to call it off. Satisfied?'

Charley digested that. As he slowed the car and swung into his short drive, she said, 'Did you get your fingers burned?'

'No.' He pressed the electronic switch on the dashboard and the garage door slid up. 'And before you ask, neither did she.'

As the car coasted in and he applied the handbrake, killing the engine, he added, 'And if you repeat any of this conversation to anyone, *ever*, I will personally strangle you.'

CHAPTER FIVE

'YOU must come to dinner again,' Geoffrey told Pierce. 'What are you doing next Saturday night?'

Pierce invented a wholly fictitious previous engagement, but Geoffrey was not to be put off. 'Give me a date when you are free, then. It needn't be a weekend.'

'It's very kind of you——'

'Nonsense. My daughter would like to see you again, I'm sure.'

Rather woodenly, Pierce said, 'Perhaps you should check that with her first.'

Geoffrey frowned. 'You haven't had a tiff, have you? The two of you seemed pretty friendly last time you were together. To be frank, I know you were kissing her before I opened the door, you know.'

Pierce regarded the floor for a moment, then lifted a steady gaze to his superior's. 'If you're asking me what my intentions are towards your daughter, Geoffrey, I feel bound to tell you that I haven't any.'

'Well—that's honest, anyway. But she isn't unattractive.'

'Of course not. She's very lovely—and very young.'

'I'll grant she's a little immature in some ways. But she's got a brain in her head. 'A's right through school and university, you know. As for the age difference, it's not that big a gap. I don't mind admitting I'd be glad to see her settle down with someone a bit older. She needs a man who can——'

'Keep her under control?' Pierce suggested drily. Then, as Geoffrey looked at him scowlingly, he said, 'I beg your pardon.

Geoffrey sighed. 'No, that's all right. I suppose it is what
I mean. I worry about her, and as a matter of fact, I did
hope that you and she——'

'I realise what a compliment you've paid me,' Pierce said
carefully.

'Yes—well. Come to dinner, anyway. No reason why you
shouldn't be friends, is there?'

Pierce gracefully gave in.

He had forgotten how stunning Trista could look. She had
put her hair up, lending emphasis to the sculpted lines of
her face, so surprising with the soft, luscious mouth and the
finely shaped brows. Her dress was almost demure, high at
the throat but leaving her shoulders bare, and belted about
her slim waist. It was a bronze colour with a slight sheen to
it, and rustled very faintly when she walked in front of him
to the lounge after opening the door.

'Dad's on the phone,' she explained. 'He shouldn't be
long. Can I get you a drink?'

She did it very competently, and he found himself
studying her, trying to analyse what lay behind the perfect
façade.

She turned with two glasses in her hands, and stood still
for a moment as she caught his gaze. He noted with interest
the hint of colour that came into her cheeks before she
crossed the room and handed him his drink.

She turned away immediately to sit down opposite him,
crossing her ankles and tucking them to one side. 'Dad says
you have a tricky case coming up.' She took a sip of her
sherry.

'Yes. I've been pretty busy preparing for it.'

She looked up briefly, then took another quick sip. 'How
busy?'

He hesitated, then said quite gently, 'Not that busy.'

'I see.' Her cheeks flamed this time, and he saw the swift rise and fall of the bronze material that covered her breasts. She lifted the glass again to her lips, licking them as she lowered it. 'I liked your sister,' she said, meeting his eyes bravely. 'She's fun.'

'Charley liked you, too.'

'She did?'

It sounded like genuine surprise. 'Why not?' he asked her.

The curve of her lip was expressive, and he said, 'I never said I didn't like you, Trista.'

'Then why——'

But her father entered the room then, apologising to Pierce. As he got himself a drink, Trista finished hers and got up. 'I'll go and check the dinner,' she said.

Pierce asked, 'Where's Mrs Kemp?'

'I'm cooking tonight,' Trista answered. 'There are only the three of us.'

It was a simple menu of halved avocados sprinkled with lemon and pepper, roast pork and vegetables, and a plate of cheeses to follow. But it was delicious, and Pierce complimented Trista sincerely afterwards.

'Thank you,' she said coolly. She had spoken little at dinner, except when directly addressed, efficiently placing the filled plates on the table and whisking them away as they were emptied, eating her own food with downcast eyes, apparently absorbed in the meal.

When she began clearing the table afterwards, he rose too, picking up some of the dishes.

'You needn't bother with that,' she said. 'Go and sit in the lounge with Dad, and I'll bring in some coffee.'

'I'd rather help,' he said, and followed her to the kitchen while her father went to the other room.

'Put them on the bench,' she said. 'Thank you.'

She switched on a coffee-making machine and began

stacking a dishwasher. 'I can manage now.'

'I'll wait for the coffee, and help you carry it through.'

He watched her get the cups, her movements graceful and sure, and when the coffee machine began to bubble he went over to check it. She was pouring wrapped dinner mints into a glass dish on the table when he said, 'It's ready,' and she looked up at him. He asked, 'Shall I pour it?'

'I'll do it.' She came over to the bench, but before she reached the counter he took her arm lightly.

'Trista——'

She jerked away. '*Don't!*'

Astonished, he stared back at her. 'I wasn't going to attack you,' he said mildly. Ostentatiously, he stepped aside for her, his eyes narrowed now as she picked up the squat glass jug and poured the fragrant liquid into the cups. She wasn't looking at him, but it gave him an odd sense of satisfaction to know that she was well aware of his gaze as it followed her every move.

She was angry with him, of course, because he had not followed up that first date. But he couldn't help contrasting the violent and instinctive repudiation of his touch with the undoubted enthusiasm with which she had welcomed his kiss before. Remembering it made his body tingle with desire as he watched her downbent head.

She replaced the jug and turned, surprising him. He saw the pupils of her eyes darken as she met his concentrated stare. Her voice a little husky, she enquired, 'Do you want cream and sugar?'

'Sugar,' he answered. 'Nothing else.'

'You'd better help yourself.' She put a little cream into the other two cups, adding a spoonful of sugar to hers.

He stood behind her. A tendril of hair curled on her nape, escaping the pins. Involuntarily, he trailed the back of two fingers up from the collar of her dress, and tucked the stray wisp in.

Almost inaudibly she said, 'Don't. That isn't fair.'

'I know,' he acknowledged, but the tacit confession only increased his desire. His hand went to her bare shoulder, shaped to his palm, and he turned her to face him. 'I'm probably going to regret this,' he muttered, and lowered his mouth to hers.

Her hands curled into fists against his chest. Her body was rigid, her mouth cool—and closed.

Almost roughly, he put his other arm about her waist and pulled her to him. With a kind of angry hunger, he forced her lips apart and gave a grunt of satisfaction as she suddenly shivered and relaxed against him, her arms coming up to lock themselves about his neck.

Exultant, he explored her mouth, enjoying the pliancy of her body in his arms, the smooth skin under his hand. He turned a little to lean against the table, spreading his thighs to hold her between them.

Perhaps that broke the mood for her. She pulled away from the kiss quite suddenly, and after a moment he let her go. The pounding blood in his veins receded a little. He saw her put an unsteady hand to her hair, tautening the material over her breasts. His eyes became riveted.

Trista dropped her hand. 'Stop it!' she said.

Pierce smiled. She might have ended the kiss, but her passion had been real. With that kind of reaction, she didn't have all the cards stacked on her side.

'Why did you do that?' she demanded.

'Frankly, I couldn't resist,' Pierce answered truthfully. 'You're a delectable piece of womanhood, Trista. And you don't need me to tell you that.'

Charley, he thought ruefully, would have had his head if she'd heard that bit of male chauvinism.

'Well, you can damned well resist it in future,' Trista said, working up a temper. 'You may think I'm available to any man who crosses my path——'

Pierce straightened. 'I've never thought that!'

She barely paused. 'Well, I'm not. And you needn't imagine you can paw me and kiss me any time the fancy takes you!'

'I did not paw you,' Pierce said evenly. 'And you enjoyed kissing me, Trista. Your pride's hurt because I took the initiative out of your hands. You like to be the one in control, don't you? Well, I've got news for you, lady. So do I.'

'You're very arrogant, aren't you?'

Pierce said, 'That makes two of us, doesn't it?' He laughed. 'Now, shall we take this coffee in before it gets cold?'

Geoffrey was watching the television news. As he took the cup from Trista he said, 'Switch it off, will you? Sometimes I think it wouldn't be such a bad thing for the human race to be wiped out. Mankind seems to have an ingrained will to destroy itself—or at least to destroy other members of the human race.'

'You've become jaded,' Trista said, taking her own cup and seating herself. 'I guess court work does that to you. Seeing the worst side of society.'

'Perhaps. It's easy to get cynical. What about you, Pierce? You're younger than I am. Do you feel human nature is basically evil?'

'I'll grant some people appear to be irredeemable. I doubt that anyone is born bad, though. John Stuart Mill—wasn't it?—said a moral tendency is not foreign to human nature. I believe that. Only sometimes it gets warped, or lost.' He glanced at Trista, and caught her eyes on him before she returned her attention to her coffee. A little later he directed a question to her and drew her into the conversation.

As he had suspected, she had intelligent opinions of her own. When at last he said, 'Time I was going. Thank you both for this evening,' she glanced at her watch with surprise.

'We enjoyed it too,' Geoffrey assured him. 'See Pierce to the door, Trista. Leave the cups. Mrs Kemp will deal with them tomorrow.' She had started to gather them up, but left them on the low table and accompanied Pierce instead.

'Thanks again,' he said, opening the door. He paused, looking down at her. 'My sister Charley is having her twenty-first birthday party next Saturday. It will be informal, a barbecue at my parents' home. She suggested I ask you to come.'

Trista said, 'That was nice of her. You can tell her you passed on the message. I'll send her a card.'

'Why not come to the party?'

'You don't really want me to.'

'Obviously I phrased it wrongly. Shall we start again?'

'That isn't necessary.'

'I think it is. I'm asking you to come to the party with me. I would like to have you there as my partner. And the fact that Charley specially suggested I should ask you assures you of being doubly welcome. She wants to meet you again.'

'And what do *you* want, Pierce?'

He said, 'That's direct.'

She stared up at him, waiting for an answer.

'I want to see you again.' He shrugged. 'Isn't that enough—for now?'

'All right,' she said at last. 'I'll come.'

'Good. I'll pick you up about six.'

'What would Charley like for a present?'

'You don't need to bring a present.'

'I'd like to get her something.'

'Well—a record, a tape, perhaps. She likes Joan Armatrading. Or—I don't know. You would probably have a better idea of what a girl your age might want than I do.'

'I'll find something.' She hesitated. 'Thank you for asking me.'

'Thank you for accepting,' he said. 'I rather expected you to turn me down flat.'

'I like your sister.'

'I suppose I deserved that.' He looked down at her, a faint smile on his mouth. 'See you Saturday, then.'

'Yes.' She stepped back from him, and his smile grew.

'Goodnight, Trista,' he said formally.

'Goodnight.'

She dressed in a red shirt and tight denim jeans for the party. A barbecue would obviously be informal. Her hair she pulled back into a ponytail and tied with a red ribbon. She was admiring the effect when Pierce arrived.

She ran to open the door before her father got there. She didn't want him dragging Pierce into the sitting-room for a chat.

Wearing a jersey shirt with a pullover and dark cord trousers, he surveyed her and said, 'You'll need a sweater or something. It's really a bit late in the year for a barbecue, but Charley insisted.'

'I've got a jacket,' she said, and fetched it, slinging it over her shoulder as she rejoined him. 'Do I meet with your approval now?'

'A leading question,' he said. 'Every time I see you, you've changed your image again.' His eyes were on the jaunty ponytail.

'Don't you like it?' She touched the ribbon as they walked down the path.

'It's fine. Very tempting, though.' He helped her into the car.

While he was going round to get into his seat, she worked

out what he had meant. As he started the engine, she said, 'I can't imagine you pulling the girls' ribbons undone at school. I'm sure you were a very well-mannered little boy.'

'*I'm* sure all the boys pulled your ribbons undone. Grown males have other ways of attracting a girl's attention. Less crude ones, I hope.'

She looked at him sideways. 'Does that mean my ribbon is safe tonight?'

He laughed down at her. 'Reverting to type, I see,' he drawled.

Trista drew back, gazing straight ahead with her chin up. 'You started it,' she said huskily.

'Hey!' He put a hand over one of hers. 'I was teasing. It wasn't a snide remark.'

'Wasn't it?' She turned to look at him.

'Promise.' His grip tightened a little, then unexpectedly he lifted her hand to his lips before replacing it in her lap and releasing it.

CHAPTER SIX

THE barbecue was set up on a wide lawn behind the house. French doors opened off a big, comfortably furnished lounge on to a wide concrete terrace, and most of the guests were sitting outside on garden chairs, or on the broad steps leading from the terrace to the lawn.

Charley came up the steps when she saw her brother and Trista arrive, and greeted them with enthusiasm.

'Come and meet my parents,' she invited Trista.

Her father was a tall, greying man with searching eyes very like his son's. He shook her hand with a firm grip and cast a quick look at Pierce. Mrs Allyn, pretty and still dark-haired, gave her a warm smile and said, 'I'm so pleased to meet you, and we're glad you came. Charley's been telling us about you.' Trista glanced at Pierce. Did that mean that he hadn't mentioned her?

She gave Charley the tapes she had bought, and caught Pierce's eyes as Charley tore off the wrapping and gave a squeal of delight.

'If you already have them, you can change them,' Trista offered.

'No, I don't yet,' Charley assured her. 'Thank you very much. I was going to buy this one. I'll put it on straight away! Pierce, look after Trista. There'll be some sausages ready soon.'

She ran lightly back up the steps, and in a few moments music competed with the sounds of people talking and laughing.

'Well, it's better than *some* of her music,' Mr

Allyn commented.

Pierce laughed. 'Charley's taste isn't at all bad,' he said, adding, 'Come on, Trista, let me get you something to drink, and I'll introduce you to my other sister later.'

She met Antonia's husband Ken, first. Large and good-looking, with curly brown hair, he gave her a friendly nod and offered a sausage on a skewer, saying, 'Get a plate or a slice of bread for her, Pierce. The poor girl looks starved.'

Trista laughed. 'Not at all. That looks good, though.'

Pierce picked up a plate from a table nearby for her and one for himself, and they ate sausages rolled in bread and dripping with tomato sauce.

Wiping her fingers on a paper napkin, she looked up and saw him regarding her rather quizzically. When she raised her brow in enquiry, he just smiled and looked away.

'There's Antonia,' he said. 'With her eldest.'

She saw a dark-haired young woman, more like Pierce than Charley, coming towards the barbecue, holding by the hand a little girl of about four. Antonia stopped by her husband, resting her hand for a moment on his shoulder. He turned to smile at her, and they exchanged a brief kiss.

The little girl caught sight of Pierce and came running over to him. 'Uncle Pierce!'

He lifted her and she flung her arms about his neck, enthusiastically kissing his cheek. 'Shane's asleep,' she told him. 'But Mummy said if I'm very good I can stay up till nine o'clock.'

'This is my niece, Kirsten,' Pierce told Trista. 'Shane is her little brother. Say hello to Trista, Kirsty.'

'Hello.' The child looked at her curiously. 'Are you

Uncle Pierce's girlfriend?' she asked.

'Don't answer that,' Pierce said, as Trista involuntarily looked to him. He was smiling. 'It's not the sort of thing to ask, Kirsty,' he explained.

Antonia came up to them. 'What's she been saying now?'

Pierce laughed. 'Never mind. Nothing dreadful. Antonia, this is Trista Vandeleur.'

'Oh?' Antonia's interested glance didn't escape Trista. They talked for a few minutes, and then Antonia took Kirsten back to the barbecue to find her something to eat.'

'Why did she look at me like that?' Trista asked.

'Like what?'

'As though—I don't know,' Trista confessed. 'As though she knew something I don't.'

'My sisters know a lot about me that you don't,' Pierce answered lightly. 'The deepest, darkest secrets of my past. That's the drawback of families. Also,' he added, as she looked dissatisfied with his answer, 'I don't bring many girls home.'

Trista considered. 'Because you don't date many, or because you prefer to keep them away from your family?'

'I've dated a few,' he said. 'I'm nearly thirty.'

'Most men of your age are married. Is your family getting anxious?'

'Not that I'm aware of. Are you asking me why I'm not married?'

'No. But why?'

'I suppose I haven't met the right girl—or woman, as Charley would insist I should say.'

'Are you choosy?'

'When it comes to marriage, yes.'

She would have liked to ask him what he was looking for,

but as she was framing the words they were interrupted by a hearty young man who seemed to be an old friend of the family, and then there was very little chance to talk to him alone. Pierce introduced her to lots of people, got her a plate of steak and salad and baked potatoes, and later a dish of fruit and cream, kept her glass filled with sparkling white wine, and even danced with her. But although she enjoyed herself Trista felt that he was treating her rather as he might a younger cousin. Except that he seemed to have no desire to cuddle her, she might have been Kirsten.

She was vaguely conscious that some of Charley's male friends had been eyeing her with interest. She was accustomed to that, and it didn't bother her. When one of them asked her to dance, she went willingly with him up the steps to the terrace where several couples were stamping and gyrating to heavy beat. Charley waved to her and grinned. 'Watch him,' she advised gaily, raising her voice above the music. 'Gordon's dancing is wild!'

'Don't listen to her,' the young man said loftily. 'She's just jealous.'

Gordon was inventive, but she found it fun trying to keep up with him. He soon saw that she could, and with a wide smile threw her a challenging look and became even more adventurous.

Trista, her ponytail swinging, laughed and followed all the way. Soon the music took her over, and she moved with it, to the drumbeat in her soul, her body flowing into it. When the beat became slower, she swayed her hips and moved her shoulders, tipping back her head to drink in the sound, eyes almost closed, only half aware of her partner, whose steps she was matching as they became less frenetic, more smoothly rhythmical.

When the tape ended, she came back to earth, giving him a languid smile as he said, 'You're great! Let's dance again.'

She shook her head. 'Later, maybe.'

He said. 'You're with Charley's brother, aren't you? Isn't he a lawyer, or something? And you're his boss's daughter, aren't you?'

'How did you know?'

'Charley said something, I think. Listen, are you—I mean, do you see other guys?'

'I might.' She looked at him from under her lashes, and he flushed and swallowed. 'Well, I wondered if you'd like to come out with me one night—or day.'

'I might,' she said again. 'Call me some time.'

'Give me your number.' He hauled a battered little diary out of his back pocket, with a pencil tucked in its spine.

'Here.' She took them from him and wrote down the number herself.

When she walked down the steps, she saw Pierce lounging on the lowest one, a glass in one hand, watching her.

'Giving him your phone number?' he enquired.

'Yes. Do you mind?'

He regarded her thoughtfully. 'Were you hoping I would?'

She was standing directly in front of him as he got to his feet. She looked into his eyes and saw laughter in them.

Angry, she said, 'I really don't care. You don't have any rights over me.'

His brows went up. 'Have I claimed any?'

Knowing that it was his apparent indifference that was making her frustrated and furious, she took a firm hold on her temper, and gave him a dazzling smile, the one that practically never failed to reduce a man to a stammering incoherent jellyfish. 'Perhaps,' she purred, looking at him in a certain way, 'I wish you would.'

To her utter chagrin, he laughed outright. Her mouth

went tight, and she stared at him with near-hatred, but he didn't seem to notice. Taking her hand, he said tolerantly, 'Come and dance with me. This is my kind of music.'

It was a trumpet solo, slow and dreamy. As he took her in his arms she was stiff, and he looked down at her with surprise. 'Are you offended with me?'

She shrugged. 'Of course not.' Making an effort, she relaxed against him, melting fluidly into his encircling arms. Her hands slid up his shirt to link behind his neck, the fingers moving into the soft hair lying on his nape. Her eyes, wide and innocent, met an enigmatic gaze that made her steps falter.

'Sorry,' she said, picking up the rhythm again. She removed her gaze and laid her head against his shoulder. He felt good, warm and strong. She thought of Kirsten snuggling up to him . . .

Lifting her head, she said, 'Do you like children?'

A smile lit his eyes, and she wished crossly that he didn't find every second thing she said funny. 'I like my niece and nephew,' he said. 'And some of the other children I know. One or two I've found pretty horrible.' He added, 'Quite a few of my friends have kids. As you pointed out earlier, most men of my age are married—with families.'

And she had asked him why he wasn't. Suddenly she felt depressed. 'I don't want to dance any more.' She pulled away from him.

'Was it something I said?' he asked humorously.

'I'm thirsty. Is there any more wine?'

'Plenty. You've had a fair bit already.'

'So?' She turned on him, a hostile glint in her eyes.

'So,' he said softly, 'are you sure you can handle any more?'

'Is that anything to do with you?'

'You're my guest——'

'I'm Charley's guest. And you're not *my* big brother!'

She glared at him, and he made her an ironic little bow. 'All right. More wine for the lady.'

Soon after he handed it to her, and she had defiantly drunk half of it in a few minutes, his father called for silence, and Charley was asked to cut a large birthday cake. Amid cheers and singing they drank a toast to her, Trista finishing her wine.

After that the world seemed brighter, and she threw herself into enjoying the party, dancing again with Gordon, and with a couple of other men, joining a cluster of young people around Charley and sharing in the laughter as they told stories about her, taking part in a game that someone decided would be fun and that involved teams of six trying to pass a lemon down the line and back without using their hands. And when Pierce caught her up and took her off with him to dance again, she flirted with him outrageously, winding her arms about his neck and holding his eyes with a brilliant gaze as she smiled up at him.

His answering smile seemed a little grim. 'Enjoying yourself?' he asked.

'Very much. Can't you tell?' The slightly muzzy feeling she had experienced after the cake-cutting had disappeared. Out of bravado she had insisted on having yet another glass of wine, but she had taken a long time to empty it, and some of it had been surreptitiously poured into a plant pot. She hoped that azaleas liked white wine.

'Let me know when you want to go home,' Pierce said.

'I may never go home. I'm having too good a time.'

'I'm glad.'

'Are you?' She looked at him with a hint of defiant scepticism.

'Why not?' he countered.

'You remind me of my father sometimes.'

'Whatever that has to do with it,' Pierce answered. 'Let

me remind you, Trista, I'm *not* your father. And I'm not your big brother, as you told me in no uncertain terms earlier.'

'Are you angry?' she asked him, half-hopefully.

'No. I'm just giving you fair warning.'

She made her eyes wide. 'Warning? Of what?'

He stopped dancing. Stopped dead. His arms locked about her, he said, 'I'm sure you know.'

Her heart gave a sudden lurch of fright. She felt heat rise to her cheeks, her breath coming faster, and she couldn't wrench her gaze away.

This is silly, she thought confusedly. He was only looking at her, for heaven's sake. She could handle men, she'd always been able to call the tune.

She laughed, annoyed that it came out a shaky little sound. 'Why, Pierce! Are you going all masterful on me?' she asked lightly. 'How thrilling!'

His reluctant smile was ironic. 'You don't scare easily, do you?'

'Why should I?' she asked confidently. 'You wouldn't hurt me.'

He was still looking down at her, and a strange expression flitted across his face.

Rather breathlessly, she added, 'Would you?'

'No,' he said. 'I wouldn't hurt you.'

He took her home in the early hours. At the door she turned to him. The streetlights were out, and his face was shadowed. 'Thank you,' she said. 'I had a wonderful time.'

He didn't move. She had a disconcerting feeling that he was going to leave without kissing her goodnight. And she wanted him to kiss her, wanted his arms about her, his mouth on hers. She put out her hand, and he took it in his. He looked down at it for a moment, before tugging her closer, lifting her hand until it rested against his heart.

His other hand went to her throat, his thumb raising her chin.

She closed her eyes, waited for the touch of his lips and, when it came, opened her mouth to him like a flower in the sun.

Their lips clung and tasted and explored, and when at last he broke the kiss he slid his hand round to her nape and drew her to him. Her head dropping against his shoulder, she flattened her hand over his heart. It was beating strongly. He felt good to her, male-scented, warm . . . safe. His fingers stroked her, lifting the ponytail, at last tugging it gently to make her look at him.

'Want to see me again?' he asked her.

'Yes,' she whispered.

He seemed to be searching her eyes in the darkness. 'No games, Trista,' he said softly. 'Not for us. You can tell Gordon when he phones that you're not available.' She stiffened slightly, and his hand closed on her nape, giving her a little shake. 'Can't you?'

She said, 'You don't have the right to give me orders.'

His hands moved again, firmly cupping her face. 'It's not an order. It's a request.' His thumbs were moving over her cheeks, shaping the bones beneath, sending her senses crazy. 'You don't care about Gordon,' he said.

'Maybe I don't care about *you*.'

His head dipped a little to one side. 'No?'

He came closer, until she was trapped against the door. His mouth came down again on hers in sweet punishment, and at first she tried to fight it, but in seconds the taste and the feel of him overwhelmed her, and she was kissing him helplessly back.

He stepped away from her and said harshly, 'Well?'

It wasn't fair, she thought. It was scary. She had never felt like this in her life. 'I . . . I'll tell him,' she said, defeated.

She saw the quick rise and fall of his chest, and thought he wasn't so sure of her. It gave her beaten pride a little boost.

'Right,' he said. 'I'll call you. Goodnight.'

She watched him go down the path. He stopped at the car and turned. His voice came clearly in the night air. 'Go inside.'

He waited there until she had closed the door behind her. Then she heard the car start and drive away.

She was restless and moody next day, made worse by her father's questions about the party, obviously aimed at discovering if she was likely to be going out with Pierce again. She didn't want to tell him, and she was nervous in case Pierce changed his mind again. He might enjoy kissing her—he had admitted that, though she hardly needed to be told in words—but he surely didn't approve of her.

When the telephone rang just after lunch, she flew to answer it.

It was Gordon. 'Oh. Hello,' she said listlessly, almost sick with disappointment.

Gordon laughed. 'You sound like the morning after,' he said. 'How about coming out with me tonight? A movie, or we could go someplace we could dance, maybe. If I can think of one.'

'No, I don't think so.'

'Aw, come on,' he coaxed.

'No, really, I don't feel like it.'

'Too much whoopee last night?' he diagnosed. 'Well, what about next Saturday, then?'

'No, sorry.'

There was a pause. 'Are you giving me the brush-off?'

When she didn't answer, he said, 'Last night you were keen enough.'

'Last night was a party,' she pointed out rather snappily.

'Yeah, well . . . sorry I asked.'

'That's all right.' She wanted to get rid of him, afraid that Pierce might find the line engaged. 'I'm sorry, too,' she managed. 'I mean, for giving you the wrong impression.'

'Oh, sure,' he answered. 'Well . . . goodbye, then.'

After that she was positively jittery. She had given Gordon her number last night, but now she didn't want to hear from him. In the cold light of day, perhaps Pierce would decide not to call her after all. Poetic justice, she admitted to herself, briefly wishing she had been nicer to Gordon. But her thoughts soon reverted to Pierce. He'd said he would call, but that was a casual promise. He hadn't said anything about when. Maybe even then, he had been giving himself a chance to get out. On the other hand, what he *had* said surely amounted to some sort of commitment? Her mind was on a see-saw, and by the time she and her father had eaten their evening meal she was in a trough of despair.

She was washing up when the phone rang again, and she ran into the hall to answer it.

'Trista,' Pierce said.

She replied coldly, 'You've taken your time.'

'Missed me, did you?' he teased, and her temper flared. 'Not a lot. You're lucky you caught me still in.'

'Oh? Where are you going?'

'Gordon called,' she said recklessly. 'Hours ago. I thought you weren't going to, so . . .'

'I see.' His voice was quite even. 'That's it, then. Enjoy yourself.'

The phone clicked in her ear, and she stared at the wall in front of her, scarcely believing that he had hung up. She put the receiver back on its cradle, and waited, willing the bell to ring. But she knew it wouldn't. Pierce would never contact her again. No games, he had said. Not between us. He wasn't like the others. He was finished with her.

Unless . . .

She felt cold and sweaty, her armpits moist, her hand shaking as it curled about the receiver and lifted it. Then she realised that she didn't know his number.

The book, she thought, fumbling as she dropped the receiver back. But she wouldn't need the book. Her father had the number, of course. He was watching television in the lounge. Quickly she went into his small study, where there was another phone, and pressed the 'A' button on the flip-up telephone index standing beside it on his desk.

The ring went through five times, and she thought, He's gone out. He'd had time to call some other girl by now, and he'd gone to meet her somewhere. She was about to hang up on the sixth ring when the phone was lifted and Pierce said 'Hello?'

Relief made her knees go weak. She sat down on the big leather chair her father used, clutching at the receiver in her hand. She couldn't speak.

Pierce said, 'Trista?'

'I'm sorry,' she offered in a small voice. 'I'm not going anywhere with Gordon. He phoned and I put him off.'

He didn't respond, and she said sharply, 'Don't hang up. Please?'

'I'm not hanging up.' He sounded as though he was thinking, his voice deep and slow.

'I thought . . . well, after the last time . . . I was afraid you'd changed your mind. I'm not making sense, am I?' she concluded mournfully.

He laughed then, softly, and her bones seemed to turn mushy. 'Not a lot,' he told her. 'Your thought processes are . . . interesting.' He added, 'I didn't think you were the type to sit by the phone waiting like Rapunzel for some man to contact you.'

'I'm not!' she said emphatically, recovering some spirit. 'That's why——'

'Ah! I see.' He paused. 'Listen, I went round early to my parents' place to help with the cleaning up after the party. There was a fair bit to do. Antonia and her family had stayed the night, since they live out of town, and when it was time for them to go they found the car wouldn't start. So I ran them home. It's almost a four-hour trip there and back, and Antonia insisted on feeding me before I left again. I've just got in. Frankly, I'm bushed. We lawyers are unaccustomed to physical labour, as my dear little sister reminded me today.'

'How is Charley?'

'Disgustingly healthy and blooming. She's still on a high from last night, in spite of going to bed at dawn. Mind you, she didn't emerge from it until almost lunchtime. By then, of course, the bulk of the work was done.'

She sat playing with the curled cord of the telephone, smiling for no particular reason, although she was still tense, her palms damp. 'I like your family,' she said.

'Good.' He sounded slightly distracted. 'Just a minute.'

Seconds later he said, 'You still there, Trista?'

'Yes. What are you doing?'

'*Now* I'm lying comfortably on my sofa with a stiff whisky. I was getting ice from the fridge when you phoned back. It had started melting all over the place.'

She pictured him on the sofa, his shoes off, the receiver cradled against his ear while he sipped his drink. 'I thought you'd called someone else,' she confided in a little rush. 'Gone out with someone else.'

She was sure she could hear the faint clink of the ice in his glass. Then he said, 'Trista—what I said last night—it cuts both ways. You know that?'

'Yes.' She had known that if he was asking for exclusivity,

he would apply it to himself as well. There had been no need to ask. But just now she had thought he was ending the relationship before it had begun. And that would have freed him of any implied obligation to her.

What he was saying was that he had forgiven her; that they could go back to where they were last night. Her death-grip on the telephone receiver relented. She breathed in deeply, then relaxed.

'Shall I come round?' he asked her.

'No. You're tired. Stay comfy.' Normally she wouldn't have cared. She would have expected any man interested in her to come rushing over if she was bored or wanted to go somewhere, and felt like having his company. That was part of the price of being allowed to date her. Pierce was different. He was tired and he didn't want to move, and the fact that he had offered was enough. Somehow it was more important that he should rest because he needed it.

'What about you?' he asked. 'Are you comfortable?'

She was swivelling her father's chair slightly, from side to side, leaning back into the buttoned leather. 'Yes. I'm fine.'

'Good.' He paused, probably taking a sip of his drink. 'Then let's talk,' he said. 'What are you doing next Saturday night?'

'Nothing.'

'OK. What would you like to do?'

Softly, she said, 'Whatever you like.'

His laugh came gently down the wire. 'The silken rope,' he said.

'What?'

'Nothing. Forget it. Now . . . shall we discuss what we'd both like to do?'

Trista gave a soft little laugh of her own, and he said, 'Behave yourself. We're going out together—so where to?'

CHAPTER SEVEN

THEY saw a lot of each other in the next two months. They attended films and shows and exhibitions together, dined out and danced, and when Trista was invited to a party she took Pierce along. He fitted in better than she would have expected, but at the same time made the boys nearer her age look impossibly young and clumsy.

Sometimes he kissed her. When he took her home after a date he would pull her to him in the car, or on the front porch, just before she let herself into the house, and kiss her until she was mindless with need, clinging to him, almost sobbing with frustration when he gently disengaged himself, even though she knew he was aroused.

After seeing a new film one evening, when the rain was pouring down and they had to run to the car, arriving breathless and laughing, Pierce offered, 'Supper somewhere? Or straight home to dry off?'

She said, wiping the rain from her face with a tissue, 'I've never been to your place.'

After a moment he said casually. 'It's not special. Just an ordinary flat.'

Trista crumpled the tissue, and pushed damp hair off her forehead. 'Do you live there alone?'

'Yes.'

'Charley stays with you sometimes, doesn't she?'

'Occasionally. She likes working in the country—driving round the backblocks with the rest of the team in a water-board truck is apparently just what she wants to do with her life. And living across the bridge and twenty minutes from

Queen Street mostly suits her. But every so often she has a
hankering for the shops and the bright lights. And if she's
late she comes to my flat, rather than take the bus home at
night.'

'She told me she finds you very useful. Your parents
don't worry about her jaunts to the city because they know
she has a safe place to stay, with you.' She paused. 'Don't
you want to take me there?'

'Why not?' He shrugged. 'But I warn you, it's not very
exciting.'

Pierce ushered Trista through a tiny hall and into the
lounge, where a tweed sofa and two rust-coloured,
comfortable velvet chairs flanked a glass-topped coffee-table
standing on an oriental rug. On one wall was an unusual art
piece, half-collage, half-painting, composed of natural wool
threads against a vibrant painted pattern like a
kaleidoscope, all sharply defined edges and points.

Pierce found her a towel, still warm from the airing
cupboard, and showed her into the bathroom.

Returning down the narrow passageway after drying
herself off and combing her hair, she peeped into two
bedrooms, one almost bare, kept for guests, obviously, and
his, with a jacket thrown down on top of the dark blue
cotton bedspread, a pair of shoes lying on the floor beside it,
one drawer of the mahogany dressing-table half open, and a
small pile of books on the bedside table.

Pierce came from the direction of the kitchen and living-
room as she stood in the doorway of his bedroom. He had
another towel in his hand. 'If I'd known you were coming,
I'd have tidied up,' he said. 'I've put the kettle on. Go into
the living-room, and switch on the heater. I'll be back with
you in a tick.'

He went into the bathroom, and a few minutes later she
heard him enter his bedroom, closing the door firmly as he

came out again. Trista was in the kitchen when he returned with his jacket off and his hair freshly combed. Her clothes had remained relatively dry under her light coat, but she had taken off her shoes at the door, because the water had splashed into them.

They had coffee, sitting in the rust-coloured chairs, and Trista curled her legs under her, snuggling into the warm velvet. It was a big chair, and Pierce suddenly smiled as he put down his cup and said, 'You look about ten years old.'

Her hair was still damp and she had lost most of her make-up. She said, looking at him, 'I'm not.'

His smile deepened. 'I know. Why did you ask me to bring you here?'

'I wanted to see where you live.'

'Well . . . do you like it?'

'It's . . . like you. Not giving much away, but . . .'

'But?' he prompted.

'No, I can't put it into words.' The chair she sat on was solid, and its high back and stuffed arms gave her a feeling of being protected, cradled in its warmth. Sometimes she felt like that with Pierce, and at other times he was unpredictable and unexpected, like the wall-hanging.

'Do I say thank you?' he asked.

'No, I should. For the coffee, and the towel.'

'All right.' He got up, took the empty cup from her hand, and pulled her to her feet and into his arms. Her heart began racing even before he bent his head to kiss her. In five minutes, she was dizzy and breathless, her eyes heavy with passion, her blood singing. He eased her away and said, 'I'd better take you home.'

'Why?' she demanded.

His look told her she knew why, and she said, 'I'm *not* a teenager, you know!'

'No, thank heaven,' he answered. 'Are you asking me to take you to bed, Trista?'

She flushed. 'I didn't say that!'

'No, and I'm not going to. Come on, I'll get your jacket for you.'

She wondered if he would have been as circumspect with any other girl.

'Are you frightened of my father?' she asked as he drove her home.

'No. And I'm not frightened of you, either,' he replied.

'Oh, that's right,' she said. 'You think I'm a man-eater, don't you?'

He laughed. 'A baby one. Tell me, if I had suggested moving to my bedroom, what would you have done?'

'Asked you to take me home,' she answered promptly, hoping devoutly it was true.

'Well, then, you've got exactly what you wanted, haven't you?' he pointed out, leaving her with nothing to say.

On their next date he took her to Antonia's home, a new, comfortable family dwelling on the outskirts of Hamilton, centre of the lush farming region of the Waikato. Antonia and Ken ran some cattle and sheep on a small block of land, but Ken also worked as an accountant in the town. Their house was on a gentle rise with a view of the river which gave the region its name, a broad, placid sweep of dark green water overhung with willows and native trees. Although it was late autumn, they were enjoying one of those last-of-the-summer days that sometimes persisted into winter, and Trista was bare-legged and wearing a light dress, with a cardigan casually tied about her shoulders in case it was needed.

'This is nice,' she commented, as she admired the view with Pierce and Antonia from a broad veranda built out from the dining area and securely fenced on account of the children. They were having coffee after lunch, relaxing on canvas chairs while Ken put Shane down for an afternoon nap and Kirsten played happily in a large sandpit in a corner of the garden.

'Yes, we find it restful,' Antonia agreed. 'But not so close that I have to worry about the children, thank goodness.'

Kirsten called to her mother to admire her handiwork in the sandpit, and Antonia moved to the rail. 'Yes, darling, that's lovely!' she said with warm admiration, adding for the benefit of the adults, 'Lord knows what it is.'

'Do you worry about them a lot?' Trista asked as Antonia turned to them again. 'I mean, there are so many things that can go wrong, aren't there?' Her eyes were on the little girl, happily shovelling sand into a lopsided heap.

'There certainly are. But you could go crazy worrying about all of them. One takes normal precautions, like good fences and fireguards, and keeping the kettle cord really short. We have the hot water turned down so it won't scald, and a stove guard so they can't pull pots down on themselves . . . Lord, I could go on! You make me realise how much having children changes your life.' She grimaced. 'Still, I wouldn't be without them—most of the time.'

'You're lucky,' Trista said.

'Yes, we are. Both of them are basically healthy, bar the odd tummy turn, and I suppose when Kirsten goes to school we can expect chicken pox and a few other unpleasant but non-fatal diseases.'

Trista said, looking down at the sandpit again, 'You'll miss her when she goes to school.'

'Yes, I will, actually. They're a lot of work, and they certainly tie you down, but in my maternal moods I think it must be awful to want children and not be able to have them.'

'There's adoption,' Pierce suggested.

'Yes, but that's not so easy these days. Lots of girls who might have given up their babies for adoption are keeping them now . . . or having abortions instead.'

'I don't suppose it's quite the same as having your own, either,' Pierce said.

Trista, who had been watching Kirsten, turned to him. 'Do you think adoptive parents don't feel the same about their children?'

'I'm not really qualified to comment. I just think it must be different,' he answered. 'Especially for a mother.'

'Yes,' Antonia said. 'But there's certainly no lack of love in the adopted families I know. Of course, it *is* different for the mother. For nine months before they were born I was bonding with my babies, they were a part of me. An adoptive mother has to start nine months late, but I guess they make up for it by wanting a child so much.'

Trista turned the cup in her hands, absently watching the play of the sunlight on the remaining liquid in the bottom.

'It must be horrendous for the natural mother, though, parting with her baby,' Antonia added, her eyes darkening with compassion. 'I couldn't do it. Now they have open adoptions, don't they?' she asked Pierce. 'Where the parents meet the mother, and let her know about the child's progress. It's better, I'm sure. Less cruel.'

Pierce said doubtfully, 'Some legal people and social workers think the old way might be better in the long run. For the child, anyway. Contact can lead to problems later, the child having divided loyalties, the natural mother fixating on the child instead of getting on with her life.'

'Oh, but——' Antonia paused as a plaintive little voice arose from the sandpit.

'Mummee! It won't stand *up*!'

'Try again, darling!' she called. To Pierce she said, 'You mean, if the mother can't let go, can't accept that the child isn't hers any longer . . .?'

'*Mummee*!' Kirsten called. 'Please, Mummy! Help me?'

'We're talking, darling,' Antonia explained patiently.

'In a little while . . .'

'I'll go.' Trista jumped up.

She put her cup on the table, and Antonia said, 'But you haven't finished——'

'It's OK.' Trista flashed her a smile. 'I've had enough.' She disappeared and seconds later they could see her crossing the grass, the full skirt of her cotton dress swinging about her legs. She knelt by the sandpit, and Kirsten raised her sand-streaked face to her.

'We've bored her,' Antonia said ruefully to her brother. 'She's very young, isn't she?'

She certainly looked it at the moment, Pierce admitted to himself, watching Trista kick off her low-heeled, plaited leather pumps, and sit on the edge of the sandpit, pulling up her skirt to show bare, tanned legs. A ponytail, tied with a wide ribbon, swung against her shoulder. Kirsten's hair was fixed in the same style. Trista picked up a small spade, and began digging in the sand while Kirsten happily directed her.

'Too young for me, you mean?' Pierce asked Antonia. He would be thirty in a few weeks.

'Are you serious about her?'

'You mean, am I thinking of marriage?'

'Well, *are* you?'

He strolled over to the rail, looking down at the sandpit. Trista was right in it now, her dress tucked into her panties, hands shaping a rapidly growing mound of sand.

'Don't get me wrong,' Antonia said. 'She seems a nice enough kid . . . and of course, she's lovely to look at.'

'Sometimes,' he said, 'I get the feeling that she stopped growing at about seventeen. She's twenty-one, Toni. A lovely, twenty-one-year-old kid.'

She didn't even object to his shortening her name. Sometimes, he thought irrelevantly, Antonia looked very like their mother. Her eyes were sympathetic, but she looked slightly bothered. 'I've never imagined you'd be happy with a child-bride,' she said frankly. 'You're the brightest of us, of our family. The most ambitious, too. And even when you were young, you had a serious streak.'

'Trista's no fool.'

'No, but . . . she doesn't exactly flaunt her intelligence, does she?'

'She's good at playing the slightly dumb blonde. I suspect that in some ways her father encouraged it. He's proud of her academic achievements, but at the same time, Geoffrey's view of women seems to run to the traditional. He thinks they should be decorative and not too assertive. A woman having brains is fine, but she shouldn't advertise the fact. I can't help wondering what Trista's mother was like.'

'I'd forgotten she's your boss's daughter.'

'I hadn't.'

Antonia blinked at him. 'You don't mean you'd marry her because of that?' She didn't believe it, she told herself, not for a minute. The trouble was that, unlike Charley, who in spite of the greater age gap seemed mostly to understand Pierce, Antonia had always had trouble divining exactly when Pierce was teasing her. Although basically reserved, he had a sense of humour that sometimes baffled her.

His expression perfectly serious, he said now, 'Not if she was buck-toothed, fat and forty, I admit. But it wouldn't be much of a hardship, really, as she is. Even a woman must see that.'

Ken came out with a cup in his hand. 'See what?' he asked, glancing with interest at the partly outraged, partly suspicious expression on his wife's face.

'That a man wouldn't find it too much of a hardship to be married to Trista.'

'I should say not!' Ken said enthusiastically. 'It's ages since I've seen such a toothsome little bit of—'

'Ken!'

'Sorry, love,' he apologised to his wife, abashed. He winked at Pierce. 'I'm trying to mend my male chauvinist ways.' He looked thoughtful. 'Are you going to marry her?'

Pierce shrugged. 'Ultimately, that's up to the lady, isn't it? I haven't asked her yet.'

A burst of laughter came from the sandpit below, and they all looked down at it. Trista was kneeling with her arm about Kirsten's waist, and Kirsten's were wound about her neck. They were both giggling uncontrollably. Whatever it was they had been building had collapsed again, but neither of them seemed to mind. Trista suddenly put both arms about the child, and hugged her close, dropping her head to put her cheek against Kirsten's.

Ruefully, Pierce added, 'Antonia thinks it would be cradle-snatching.'

Kirsten tired of playing in the sand, and wandered away to ride her tricycle. Trista sat on the low wooden wall that surrounded the pit, her feet still half-buried in the stuff, and looked through the wire-mesh fence down the long slope, dotted with a few houses and stands of trees, to the river.

A shadow fell across her shoulder, and she looked up to find Pierce regarding her with an expression that she decided was faintly disapproving.

'Come on,' he said, holding her shoes. 'Would you like to go for a walk? There's a foot-track we can take to the river.'

'Will I need those?' She took the hand he offered to her and stood upright on the springy grass.

'Part of the way is stony.'

'I'd better wash my feet then, first.'

There was a tap by the short flight of steps to the back door, and he waited while she turned the water on her feet. Antonia came to the door with a towel and a small container of baby powder. 'Use that,' she said. 'It'll help your shoes on afterwards, and get rid of any leftover sand.'

Pierce took them from her as Trista sat down on the third step and held out her hand for the towel. Ken called Antonia from inside, and she said, 'Coming!' and ran back into the house.

'I'll do it,' Pierce told Trista, seating himself just below her, and lifting a foot on to his knee, where he had spread the towel.

He dried both her feet carefully and sprinkled talcum over them, smoothing it over her toes with his hands, his thumb moving in between them to brush away the last grains of sand.

Trista. She watched his hands on her skin, firm and gentle, and tried to breathe normally. He seemed to be concentrating entirely on her feet, as efficiently and almost impersonally as if he were dealing with one of the children.

He placed her feet side by side on the step, lifted the towel from his knees and shook it out. 'You smell like a baby now,' he commented, looking up at her wryly as he grasped her ankle and slid a sandal over her toes.

She waited while he put the other shoe on for her. Then he stood up, holding out his hand.

As she took it and got up, he said, 'Do me a favour, will you?'

Unsure of his mood, not understanding his faintly long-suffering expression, she stood mutely looking up at him.

'Let your hair out of that ponytail,' he said. 'Please.'

She pulled the ribbon off and shook it out. 'Better?'

'Slightly,' he answered. 'Shall we go? Unless you want the bathroom first.'

She shook her head, and her hair swung against her shoulders. 'I should comb my hair, though.'

'It looks fine. Come on.'

'Antonia knows we're going?'

'Yes. I offered to stay and look after the kids while she

and Ken went out for a bit, but she told me she's tired, and would like to lie down for a while. She hasn't said anything, but I think she may be pregnant again.'

He opened the gate for her, checking that it was properly shut behind them.

Trista said, 'Does she want a big family?'

'I've no idea. She's never discussed it with me.'

'I think I'd like a big family. More than one or two, anyway.'

'Didn't you enjoy being an only child?'

'It was all right, I suppose. I know other children were jealous sometimes, because . . . well, because my dad gave me nice clothes and toys, and lots of attention. At least until I went to boarding-school. Dad thought it would be good for me. I suppose it was, and some things I enjoyed, like being with girls of my own age most of the time. I'm still friendly with a few of them. But most of the time, I *hated* it.'

Surprised at the passion in her voice, he slipped an arm about her shoulders as they walked at the edge of the road, alongside a shallow ditch filled with ferns and tufts of grass. A bird erupted in a flurry of wings from under the ferns, and flew across their path. Trista started, and Pierce's hand tightened on her shoulder.

A herd of cattle in a paddock bordering the path came trotting to the fence and hung their heads over the barbed top wire to inspect the passers-by with shining blue-black eyes. Trista put a hand out to pat a pink nose, and the animal snorted in an offended way and tossed its head, trotting off to the middle of the paddock, followed by the others.

They had to climb a stile to get to the riverbank, and walk over uneven ground, pitted by hooves and covered in long, springy grass. Down near the water it was easier to walk on, perhaps smoothed by recent floods. They sat under a leafless willow on a long-fallen log and contemplated the water, which was almost motionless except for a quiet, rippling eddy here and there. Reeds growing near the edge rustled faintly as a breeze wended through them.

Pierce had held her hand to help her over the holed ground, and he retained it in his warm clasp. She was very conscious of him beside her, of the exact height of his shoulder in relation to hers, of his breath stirring her hair when he turned his head to look at a different part of the view, of the faint scent of his body, his clothes and his skin, the soap he used, perhaps an aftershave lotion.

'Do you use aftershave?' she asked him.

He looked down at her. 'Sometimes. Why? Is that a hint?'

'No.' She looked up at him. He was very close, and she felt a sudden wild urge to pull his head down to hers and make him kiss her. 'No,' she repeated huskily. 'You always smell nice.'

'Thank you, Trista.' He turned away from her, contemplating the secret depths of the river, and the lush green grasslands on the other side with their browsing cattle and red-roofed farmhouses.

She looked at the water too, wondering why he hadn't kissed her. She was sure he must have seen the invitation in her eyes. For a moment he had looked . . . tempted. But apparently the temptation was easy to resist.

Kisses, even passionate, intimate kisses of the kind that heated her blood, were only a prelude to the kind of lovemaking she increasingly longed for. She couldn't help wondering why he didn't ask for more from her. Whether, because of her father, he hesitated to involve her too deeply. Or whether, really, he wasn't all that interested, and preferred to keep their relationship on a superficial level.

That frightened her, because she knew she was in love with him, terribly, heedlessly in love for the first time since she was barely sixteen and her hormones had been rioting out of control, bringing bewildering emotional needs that she didn't know what to do about, and that she had expected—hoped—never to experience with quite that intensity again. She wanted him as she had never wanted any man before, even her very first love, who now seemed a poor fish indeed, compared with Pierce.

Unable to bear his nearness any longer, she got up and walked along the bank a little way, stopping when she reached a tree with branches that overhung the water, preventing her from going farther. Pierce watched her. She could feel his eyes on her. She clutched at a bare, whippy branch, running her fingers along the little nodes that in spring would unfold new green leaves. A wisp of smoke rose from the chimney of one of the houses across the river.

After a while Pierce came to join her. 'What are you looking at?' he asked her.

'Nothing. I'm thinking.'

'Deep, dark thoughts to match the river?' he enquired lightly.

Impatiently, she turned on him. 'I'm not a child, Pierce!'

His eyes narrowed a little, slipping over her. 'No, you're not,' he drawled. 'I had noticed that, in spite of what my sister says.'

'Antonia? What did she say?'

'That you're a nice kid. She thinks I'm too old for you.'

'It's none of her business!'

'True,' he acknowledged. 'But that's one of the drawbacks of *not* being an only child. My sisters do tend to take something of an interest in my love-life, I'm afraid.'

'Am I your love-life, Pierce?'

After the briefest hesitation, he answered, 'At the moment.'

With an effort, she lifted her chin high, kept her face from crumpling in disappointment. 'I see.'

'Do you, indeed?' He was searching her eyes, a smile

lurking in his. It wasn't an unkind smile, but it irked her, all the same.

'Let me know when you find my successor, won't you?' she asked.

'Trista,' he chided her, 'don't be silly!'

'I suppose,' she said, 'it won't be a "kid" next time. It'll be a woman—and you won't stop at kisses with her——'

He said, 'Trista!' and caught at her arms, giving her a little shake. 'Stop it, you little idiot.'

Trista took a deep, shaking breath. Pulling away from him, she gave him a blind, brilliant smile. 'Sorry!' she said. 'I guess I got a little carried away. Do *you* think that I'm too young for you?'

'Frequently.'

She looked at him consideringly. 'It's not such a big gap.'

'Nearly nine years.'

'That's nothing. Lots of couples have a bigger age difference.'

'I know. It isn't so much a matter of age . . .'

'Then I don't know what it is. My father . . .'

'Yes?' he encouraged her as she hesitated.

'My father would be thrilled to bits, if we were married—you know that, don't you?'

'Yes, I do know that.'

'He . . . he could do you a lot of good, couldn't he? If you . . . if he wanted. They'll probably make him a judge soon.'

Pierce nodded. 'Yes, they probably will. It's certainly expected before long.'

'He said you'd want to be a Queen's Counsel some day.'

'Most barristers have that ambition.'

'Well, he could help. Couldn't he?'

'Very probably. What are you trying to say, Trista?'

She looked him full in the eyes. 'My father wants us to get married.'

'And you?' he asked. 'Do you want us to get married?'

She swallowed, feeling her cheeks beginning to burn, but she wouldn't look away. She wished she could read what was in his eyes. He wasn't laughing now. He looked intent and grave, but there was something else there, too, something that might have been surprised admiration. She hoped it was, because she didn't see any love, any passion, any joy in what she was saying. 'Yes,' she said. 'I . . . would like that.'

He smiled then, but she was still tense, praying that he wasn't going to snub her, one part of her brain appalled at what she was doing, laying her heart on the line for a man, something she had sworn never, ever, to do.

'I'm . . . glad,' he said, 'that you think so much of me. But would you be happy with a husband who had married you for what he could get out of your father?'

Trista closed her eyes. She had insulted him. Of course he wouldn't marry her. He didn't love her enough for that. He had a sort of affection for her, and she could arouse his passion to a certain point, but it had never been enough to make him lose his head. Her father had thrown her at him, and he wanted to please Geoffrey, so he had asked her out against his better judgement, but there must be limits. A man like Pierce would hardly marry just to advance his career.

But she wanted so desperately not to lose him. She could have made him love her, she thought. She could. Without hope, she answered his question. 'Yes,' she said, opening her eyes, meeting his again. 'Yes, if the man is you. And,' she added, playing her trump card, 'it wouldn't be only for that, would it?'

Her gaze challenged him, and his mouth quirked. 'No,' he admitted. 'It wouldn't be only for that.'

'Well, then?'

He gazed at her in silence, and she felt like screaming at him to put her out of her suspense.

Then at last he said slowly, 'All right, Trista, if you're sure that's what you want . . . we'll get married.'

CHAPTER EIGHT

GEOFFREY very nearly beamed at the news. He enfolded Trista in a hug and almost reduced Pierce's hand to jelly. Charley was ecstatic, her parents quietly pleased; Ken had been frankly delighted and Antonia, trying to swallow her doubts, had kissed Trista's cheek and congratulated her brother with as warm a smile as she could muster. There was a hint of laughter in Pierce's eyes as he thanked her.

Geoffrey insisted on an engagement party, held on Pierce's birthday. Pierce had bought Trista a ring, a square-cut emerald flanked by two small diamonds, which she showed proudly to anyone who asked. She was wearing a shimmering dress that appeared green or silver depending on the light. It exposed a lot of leg and made her resemble a naiad, with her hair loose and brushed to a smooth sheen except for the curling ends. Her eyes sparkled and her hands moved gracefully as she talked. Sometimes she would shake back the shining fall of hair, laughing. Now and then she cast a sideways glance at her new fiancé, a look both provocative and proprietary. Once when he was talking to a rather attractive young woman she came up to him silently to hook her hand into his arm. Pierce slid his hand into hers and stood lightly holding it while he carried on speaking.

Pierce found himself receiving odd looks from young male guests, compounded of varying degrees of envy, respect and sympathy. He accepted their formal congratulations with equanimity.

When the party was over, Geoffrey discreetly left them alone. Trista seated herself on a long sofa and leaned back on the cushions. 'Come and sit down,' she invited Pierce, lifting a hand to him.

He was near the door, after saying goodnight to Geoffrey, and for a moment he didn't move. Trista dropped her hand. 'What's the matter?'

He smiled then. 'Just admiring the view.'

She glanced down at her dress. 'Do you like it?'

'Very much. Didn't I tell you that you look beautiful?' He walked towards her.

'Yes, but actions speak louder than words.' She cast him a seductive peep from under her lashes.

Halting before the sofa, he laughed softly, shaking his head. 'Trista, you are incorrigible!'

Trista jumped up. 'Don't laugh at me!' she stormed, and turned to leave him.

Pierce snatched her wrist. 'Hey!'

He spun her to face him and, furious, she raised her free hand, a closed fist thudding hard against his chest.

He captured that hand too, and, when she tried to pull away, clipped them both behind her. She whipped her head to one side, and he said, 'Come on, Trista. It's what you want.'

She set her teeth and stubbornly tried to wriggle out of his hold, but he tightened his grip and said again, 'Come on!'

Still she wouldn't face him. He bent his head, and his lips feathered her cheek. 'Trista . . . It's what I want, too,' he whispered.

She turned her head until her eyes met his, her expression still mutinous. He wasn't smiling now. His gaze dropped to her mouth. Her lips parted, and briefly his eyes glittered again into hers, before he bent slowly to take her mouth under his.

I love him, she thought, oh, how I love him! before the whole world disintegrated into little spinning pieces of light, and she was swept into the vortex.

Her head bent back under the searching pressure of his mouth, and she tried to free her hands. Finding them still imprisoned, she gave a little moan of protest, and he shifted his grip, cradling her head in his palms, his fingers in her hair. Her arms went round him, her hands under his jacket, feeling the warmth of his skin beneath the white shirt.

Without breaking the kiss, he took her down on to the sofa with him, lifting her legs across his knees as he pressed her back against the cushions in one corner. His hand skimmed her breast, and she arched herself against him and tugged impatiently at his shirt, trying to free it from his trousers.

He groaned suddenly, and sat up, pulling her on to his lap and holding her head against his shoulder.

She could feel the rise and fall of his chest. His breathing was as fast as hers, she noted with satisfaction. His voice deep and thick, he said, 'You're a temptress, my darling.'

Something inside her turned liquid and warm. It was the first time he had called her darling. She lifted her head a little, and pressed a kiss to his throat. She could see the hurried beat of a pulse there, and she placed her finger on it. Trailing her finger down to the top button of his shirt, she deftly flicked it open, and then undid the next one too.

Pierce caught her hand in his. 'No,' he said.

She looked up at him.

'There's a certain point beyond which it's very difficult to stop,' he said.

She knew that, of course. Obviously he hadn't yet come

anywhere near it. She said, 'Perhaps I don't want to stop.'
Actually, in theory she had every intention of waiting for
their wedding night, but it was galling that Pierce seemed
always to be the one to call a halt. Just once she would have
liked to be calling the shots.

'I've never fancied a shotgun wedding, myself. And
lovemaking on a sofa doesn't have a great deal to
recommend it.'

'Have you tried it often?' She looked him in the
eyes.

Pierce smiled slightly. 'Often enough to know I don't like
it much.'

He had released her hand, and her finger fiddled with the
button she had just undone. 'I want to ask you something,'
she said.

'What?'

'Dad asked you to come early tonight, so that you two
could talk while I was getting ready.'

'Yes.'

'What did you talk about?'

'You, mostly. He wanted to ensure that his ewe lamb was
going into good hands, I think. He offered some financial
assistance to see us into a nice home, if I wanted it. I'm
afraid I said no.'

'Did you?' She looked up.

He smiled. 'Surprised?'

Trista shook her head. Accepting money was a bit
different from expecting career assistance from his father-
in-law, she supposed. 'I'm glad you said no, though.'

'Sure? You realise I may not be able to keep you quite in
the manner to which you're accustomed?'

'That doesn't matter.' Her father had already warned her
that Pierce's salary wasn't equal to his, and that she mustn't
expect him to be able to provide all the luxuries that
Geoffrey had.

Her eyes returning to the tiny button in her fingers, she said, 'What else did he say? About me?' Pierce regarded her consideringly, and she raised her eyes again to his. 'What?' she insisted.

Geoffrey had said, 'I'm afraid I've spoiled her but . . . she's a good girl. A little wayward, I'll grant, and she can be remarkably stubborn. Accustomed to getting her own way, I warn you, but I'm sure you'll handle that. If you'd known her as a child—she was lovely, really lovely. A great comfort to me after my wife . . . Basically she has a very sweet nature.' He had cleared his throat. 'I know she's a bit of a flirt. With her looks, I suppose it's only natural to . . . trade on them a bit. But she's been brought up with a sound moral sense. She'll settle down, I'm sure.'

Pierce certainly wasn't going to repeat all that. He said, 'Nothing I didn't already know.'

'Nothing?' She searched his eyes.

Pierce smiled. 'Nothing,' he assured her. 'No dark secrets of your past. He didn't even show me a nude baby photo,' he teased. 'I was direly disappointed.'

She dropped her hand to her lap, curling it to run her thumb over the smooth nails. 'You don't know everything about me,' she said.

'I don't suppose I do. No doubt we'll both learn a lot about each other, once we're married. It's part of the charm of wedded bliss, they tell me.'

She took a deep breath. 'There are things you might prefer to know beforehand,' she said. 'For instance, no matter what impression my father gave you, you're not getting a virgin bride . . . sorry.'

'I didn't really expect it,' he said evenly. 'I . . . don't have the right to, for one thing.'

Determinedly, she opened her mouth again, starting to say, 'But I . . .'

Pierce put a finger across her lips. 'I've no intention

of telling you all about my past loves. And I certainly don't expect to hear the details of yours. Forget it. I promise you my total fidelity in the future, and expect yours. That's all that matters.'

'Some people don't even expect that after marriage, nowadays,' she said, as he removed his constraining finger.

'Well, I have some old-fashioned ideas,' he told her, and tipped her chin to hold her eyes with his. There was no laughter in them now; they were a little stern. 'OK?'

'Yes,' she said unhesitatingly. Geoffrey had talked to her about Pierce, too. 'He's a solid young man. He has real values and principles.' She gathered that his values and principles were ones that her father shared. Doggedly, she persisted, 'But . . .'

'No buts,' Pierce said. His lips came down again on hers, and after a few moments she slid her arms about his neck and gave herself up to the rocketing, dizzy delight of his kiss.

'Trista would like you to be a bridesmaid,' Pierce told Charley. 'She wants you and one of her university friends who's living in Wellington at the moment, so you'd have most of the work to do, whatever that entails. She asked me to sound you out, in case you minded.'

Charley was thrilled. 'I don't mind at all!'

The wedding was going to be a big affair, Pierce could see, and he resigned himself to it. Geoffrey was unstoppable. Trista had asked Pierce if he wouldn't rather have something more modest by way of celebration, but he said tolerantly, 'You're his only daughter. He wants to give you a proper wedding with all the trimmings. Let's not spoil it for him.'

'You'll go along with anything Dad suggests, then?'

she asked.

Pierce shrugged. 'I don't mind keeping him happy. Unless you have a rooted objection to a big wedding?'

'Oh, no!' she said, with the faintest hint of irony that he appeared not to notice. 'Whatever you and Dad decide is fine.'

Charley threw herself into the preparations with gusto. The wedding was to be in spring, and Charley and Trista's Aunt Hester seemed determined to make it the event of the season. Pierce discovered that Trista had few relatives. Hester, Geoffrey's only sister, was childless, and they had lost touch with her mother's family after she had died.

'What's happened to your feminist principles?' Pierce teased Charley, when after spending a day in the city she had spread his living-room carpet with bridal magazines and samples of materials. 'I thought the New Woman didn't believe in all this?'

'Romance is coming back,' she assured him. 'Even feminists believe in marriage if it's a true partnership. You're not going to be the kind of husband who thinks he owns his wife, are you?'

'Heaven forbid,' Pierce said politely. 'I promise to be a truly liberated husband.'

'Well, you can cook anyway.' Charley, having been the beneficiary of his culinary skills, knew what she was talking about. 'And this place,' she added, giving the flat a cursory inspection, 'doesn't seem too bad for a bachelor pad. You're quite house-trained, really, aren't you?'

'Probably more so than Trista,' he suggested.

'Oh!' She had clearly not thought of that. 'They have a housekeeper, don't they? Well, you're not to go all male and horrible if Trista turns out to be no good at that sort of thing.'

'I wouldn't dream of it. And she can cook.'

Charley sat back on her heels, clutching a picture of a retinue of bridesmaids dressed, as far as Pierce could see, like fairy-tale milkmaids. 'Pierce,' she said hesitantly, 'you *are* in love with Trista, aren't you?'

Pierce, lounging in one of the rust-brown armchairs, remained poker-faced, his eyes slightly narrowed. 'What's brought this on?' he asked. Charley and Trista had been close lately, what with the wedding preparations and the similarity in their ages.

'Nothing,' Charley said hastily. 'It's just that sometimes you seem . . . distant. And she seems . . . well, a little desperate. Oh, I know it's none of my business, but I don't like to see Trista hurting . . .'

'What makes you think she is?'

Charley bit her lip. 'Intuition, I suppose. Don't laugh.' She gazed at him earnestly, a little flushed, but he wasn't laughing. His gaze had sharpened as he waited for her to go on.

In a little rush, she said, 'I know she baits you—those sharp-edged little remarks she makes sometimes, that don't *seem* to be anything more than teasing, even while she's hanging on your arm or giving you one of those come-hither looks of hers that make Mum positively blush. It's because she's unsure of you, Pierce.'

'Did she say that?' he enquired.

'*No*! She hasn't said anything to me. But . . . you don't act much as though you're head-over-heels, Pierce. And it isn't *fair* to marry a girl if you don't love her.'

Pierce contemplated her thoughtfully. Charley was constantly surprising him. 'Lots of marriages are contracted for other reasons than being head-over-heels, as you put it. Maybe that isn't what Trista needs from me.'

Charley frowned in a troubled way.

'Don't worry about it, infant,' Pierce urged, leaning over to ruffle her hair. 'No one on the outside can really know a lot about the relationship between a man and a woman.' He stood up. 'How about a last cup of coffee? Trista and I are out househunting again tomorrow, and I need an early night.'

He had been surprised at Trista's preferences. She turned out to like big, roomy houses with lots of outdoor space, and if there were trees her eyes would light up.

'You like trees?' he asked her.

'Don't you?'

'Well, yes. They're not a top priority, though.'

'I think they're important,' she said. 'Children love trees—to climb, and swing from, and make tree-houses . . . and all that,' she added lamely, her cheeks flushing as she met his amused eyes.

'You're really taking this marriage business seriously, aren't you?' he asked her.

'It *is* serious, isn't it?'

'Yes, but it's early days yet to be thinking of swings and tree-houses.'

'You do want children, don't you, Pierce? You're awfully good with them.'

'Yes, of course I want children,' he assured her. 'But I'm not in a tearing hurry. Are you? I can't imagine you wanting to be tied down to babies too soon.'

She said vaguely, 'I thought we should be looking ahead, that's all.'

'OK,' he agreed. 'We'll look ahead. You like this place?'

'Yes. I know it needs some work, but we—you could afford that, couldn't you?'

'We could,' he said firmly. 'I'll get someone to check it over, and then we'll see.'

They were invited to the McGregors' for dinner. Pierce watched, intrigued, as Trista took the baby in her arms and for five minutes seemed oblivious to everyone else in the room.

'You're not listening, Trista!' he accused her when for the third time she had answered an absent, 'Mm,' to something Calum had said.

'Oh, sorry.' She flushed guiltily, and Calum laughed. 'Just wanted to know if you'd like a sherry,' he repeated. 'Or something else.'

Trista declined, her eyes on the baby. 'No, thanks. Oh, look, she's smiling at me!'

Jennifer, having inspected her with great solemnity, had apparently decided she was a friend.

Calum shook his head. 'The girl's besotted,' he told Pierce sorrowfully. 'We'll get no sense out of her for the next twenty minutes. They take some women like that.'

On their way home, Pierce said to her, 'You like babies.'

'I haven't actually had much to do with them.'

Pierce grinned. 'That was obvious the first time you met Jennifer. You seem to have got over your nervousness with her, though.'

'She's lovely,' Trista said wistfully. 'Isn't she?'

'I'm afraid they're all much of a muchness to me,' Pierce apologised.

'Oh, you won't say that when you have one of your own.'

'So my friends keep telling me.' He cast her a curious sideways glance. 'Funny, you certainly didn't strike me as a girl who'd go gaga over babies.'

'I'm not gaga!' she snapped. 'Jennifer happens to be a particularly sweet baby. And maybe you're not really such a great judge of character.'

Pierce's brows went up. 'Sorry! It was just a passing remark.' Changing the subject, he asked, 'What are you going to do with yourself after the wedding? At the moment, I gather the preparations and planning are taking a good deal of your time.'

'I'll have the house to care for. Decorating and so on.'

'It should pretty well be all done by the time we move in,' he said. 'You'll get bored, I should think.'

'Do you want a working wife?'

'I don't particularly care, one way or the other. I want a happy wife. I thought you'd want a job to occupy your time, if nothing else.'

'Mrs Kemp says that housekeeping properly is a full-time job.'

'Well, she should know. But . . . is that what you want?'

'I have a lot to learn.'

Pierce chuckled.

'What?' Trista demanded, rather suspicious.

'Just something Charley said. Well, when the novelty wears off, we'll work something out between us.'

'By then we might . . .'

'We might . . . what?'

'We might have a baby. That would certainly keep me busy!'

'It would indeed,' Pierce answered cheerfully. 'Just remember that a five-minute cuddle with Jennifer at her best, all bathed and ready for bed, doesn't give you any idea of how much work is really involved in being the mother of an infant.'

'You're not a latent paedophile, are you?' Trista shot at him.

She might have succeeded in shocking him, she hoped. If not shocked, he was certainly surprised. The car slowed as his brows went up. 'I beg your pardon?'

'I asked . . .'

'Yes, I heard. Why?'

'Because you seem determined to keep treating me as though I'm a child. I'm twenty-one, not twelve, and if I'm old enough to marry you, I'm certainly old enough to have children by you. And I do know that being a mother isn't just one long, wonderful picnic.'

The car picked up speed, but only for a few minutes. He drove into a side street, parked and turned to her, unclipping his seat-belt, and hers. 'All right,' he said. 'Fair comment. One of the things an engaged couple should work out, I suppose, is when they plan to start their family. So . . . how soon *do* you want to start?'

'I . . . well, if you want to wait, that's OK. But not too long, please?'

'But your choice would be . . .?'

'I don't care. As soon as . . . it happens.' Almost fiercely, she said, 'I *want* children, Pierce. I want a *baby*.'

He stared at her thoughtfully. 'Even though you admit you've had very little to do with them?'

'Until I met you. I love Kirsten, Pierce. And Shane, of course. You do, too. Don't you envy your sister and Ken?'

'Not wildly, no. Part of the charm of my niece and nephew is that I can always hand them back to their parents when I've had enough. Don't look like that,' he added, as Trista swallowed her disappointment. 'We'll have our own, or course we will. I just didn't know you were breaking your neck for it. Most couples prefer a little time to adjust to each other first.' Unable to see her averted face, he asked, 'Has seeing Jennifer brought this on?'

'No!' She looked up at him. 'It isn't something I've decided on the spur of the moment. Honestly.' She added, 'Dad would love a grandchild . . . grandchildren. We're his only chance.'

A faint frown appeared between his brows. 'Tell me something,' he said. 'Did you . . . decide to marry me just so that I could give you a baby?'

Her gaze was wide and innocent. 'No more,' she said, 'than you decided to marry me just because Dad could get you made a Queen's Counsel.'

His mouth quirked. 'Well,' he said, 'that's put me in

my place.'

'Maybe you needed it,' Trista said tartly.

'Peace.' He bent and kissed her lightly on the lips. 'I apologise for treating you like a juvenile. I know you're not, really. But sometimes you look so damned young that I forget.'

'Don't you like the way I look, then?' she asked pertly, reverting to her usual manner.

Pierce grinned. 'Don't fish, brat. I'm taking you home.'

CHAPTER NINE

PIERCE turned to watch his bride walk up the aisle on her father's arm.

She was preceded by the two bridesmaids in pink, and Kirsten looking important in a long organdie dress like candy-floss.

He was glad Trista wasn't wearing a veil, because he thought he had never seen anything quite so lovely. She had put her hair up, but not too severely; there were rather endearing little tendrils apparently escaping from the topknot that was encircled with tiny palest pink rosebuds. Her dress had the merest hint of pink about it too, deepening in the folds of the full skirt. She looked demure and very slightly frightened, and he smiled as she reached his side, silently reassuring her.

He took her hand in a firm clasp as they stood before the minister. Charley deftly removed Trista's small bouquet at the right time and, when the ceremony was completed, adjusted the bride's short train for their progress down the aisle. Pierce gave her a quick smile, and she grinned back. She had been the first to embrace them both when they went to sign the register. He had to stop being surprised at her efficiency, he reminded himself, stop thinking of her as his baby sister. She was the same age, very nearly, as his wife.

Who still looked a bit tense, he saw as they reached the door and stopped while the official photographer arranged the bridal party for the photographs. He tightened his grip on her hand. 'All right?' he asked her quietly.

She looked up and nodded. The photographer called, 'Smile, please!' and she obeyed. Pierce, too, went through the motions. It seemed an age before they were free to enter the car Geoffrey had hired, and subside into seats covered with slippery white satin.

'Relax,' he advised her, and put an arm about her shoulders.

She rested her head against him, sighing. 'Tell me I'll never have to do this again.'

'I've certainly no intention of allowing it.'

'We've still got the reception to go through.'

'Is it such an ordeal?'

'Yes. Why didn't we just run away? Elope?'

'Because it would have broken your father's heart. And deprived your aunt and my young sister of many hours of enjoyment.'

She sat up. 'Yes. I'd forgotten that,' she said with heavy irony.

'Wait until it's Charley's turn,' he suggested. 'You can get your own back.'

Somewhat to his relief, she laughed then. When they arrived at the reception grounds and had to endure more posing for photographs, she seemed to be actually enjoying herself, helping the photographer to pose Kirsten, and cuddling close to her so that Antonia, wearing a leaf-green maternity dress, could get an informal shot of the two of them together.

'One with you too, Pierce,' Antonia ordered, and he obliged with good grace, only muttering just for Trista's ears. 'My sister, *mein Fuhrer*!' which made her laugh, and Antonia, satisfied, called, 'Oh, a great shot!'

Trista caught her husband's eye and threatened to dissolve into giggles.

'Come on,' he said sternly, determined to forestall any manifestation of regrettably juvenile tendencies in his bride in front of her elder sister-in-law. 'You need a glass of wine and some food. You're getting light-headed.'

She felt more than light-headed later that night, when they had been shown to the honeymoon suite of a top hotel. At the reception she had drunk quite a lot of the excellent champagne Geoffrey had provided for their guests. But by the time she had showered and talcumed her body and dressed herself in a low-necked black lace nightgown, dabbed some perfume behind her ears and brushed her teeth and her hair, the pleasantly muzzy feeling had dissipated, leaving her alternately apprehensive and hot with a breathless excitement.

Pierce was sitting by the window when she emerged, his jacket slung over the back of the chair, his shirt undone. He had opened the curtains a little and was looking out at the city lights. The room was high up, and the view unobstructed. She saw the bed had been turned down.

When he heard her come in he looked at her, and she saw his eyes crinkle before his mouth quirked in a smile. 'I thought white was traditional,' he remarked, inspecting her rather thoroughly.

'Do you mind?' She hoped he wasn't disappointed. 'I look sickly in white. Besides, its . . . kind of insipid.'

'I don't mind. You look . . . fabulous. And very seductive.'

She said, 'That was the idea.' Annoyingly, her voice had turned husky, with a slight crack in it.

Pierce's smile deepened as he stood up.

She wanted to fling herself into his arms and bury her head against his shoulder, but nerves rooted her to the spot. Silly, she told herself. It wasn't as if it was the first time . . .

He walked slowly towards her. The blatant admiration in his eyes gave her a little confidence, and she managed a smile, not quite up to the standard of the one that generally brought men to her feet.

'You're lovely,' he said. The back of his hand touched her cheek, stroked down her neck to her shoulder, and followed the low neckline, resting lightly against her breast.

Trista instinctively raised her own hand and caught his in it.

Pierce smiled. Lifting their linked hands, he kissed her fingers, still holding her eyes, with a quizzical expression in his.

'Are you nervous?' he asked her, surprised.

'I've never been married before.'

'Neither have I,' he said. 'Tired?'

She could say she was . . .

She swallowed. 'No, not really. Not now.'

'Good.' He sounded crisp and decisive. He kissed her forehead briefly, then led her over to the chair he had vacated and sat her down in it. His lips brushed her cheek, slid lightly over her mouth to the other cheek. Then he straightened, crossed to the door and switched off the main light. A lamp with a rose-coloured shade on the bedside table was on dim. He took a dark robe from the foot of the bed, and said. 'Don't move. I won't be long.'

She watched him close the bathroom door, and then turned her attention to the view.

She didn't look round when he came out ten minutes later. The carpet was too thick for her to hear him walking across it, but she knew when he was standing behind the chair, and her breath quickened.

He moved her hair aside with his fingers, and pressed his lips to her nape. His hand caressed her neck and her shoulder, his thumb slipping under the thin strap of the nightgown and moving back and forth. His lips were warm on her shoulder, and she tipped back her head as he placed a kiss in the hollow of her neck.

He lifted his head and whispered in her ear, 'Trista . . . are you ready for bed?'

She nodded, her eyes closed.

His other hand took hers where it lay in her lap, and he drew her up into his arms. She raised her mouth blindly for his kiss, and met it with passionate abandon. When his gentleness broke and his lips became hard and searching, she shivered in anticipation.

Pierce drew back, breathing hard. His thumb feathered across her lips. 'All right?' he asked, his voice low.

'Yes. Pierce . . .' she whispered back, clinging to him, her body on fire under the film of lace, absorbing the heat of his. 'I want you!'

She heard the fierce intake of his breath, felt it too. 'You are stunning,' he said soberly, his hand stroking her shoulder, skimming on down her arm. 'Quite stunning. Come on, darling, let's go to bed.'

'Yes,' she murmured. 'Please.'

He picked her up in his arms and carried her the few short steps to it.

They travelled south the next day, stopping for lunch at Rotorua, looking out over a vista of steaming hot pools at Whakarewarewa, and catching a good view of Pohutu geyser in eruption being snapped by a busload of Japanese tourists.

'Want to walk round?' Pierce asked her, but Trista shook her head. She had seen it all before.

'I actually prefer the lakes,' she said, 'although when I was a child, of course, the boiling mudpools fascinated me. I remember dragging Daddy back to the "frog-pond" down there several times. I was nearly convinced those spurts of mud plopping about in it were really frogs.' Catching the smile in his eyes, she added drily, 'I've grown out of that.'

They were heading for the largest lake of all, the inland sea
right in the centre of the island, that the Maori had named
Taupo-nui-a-Tia, 'the Great Cloak of Tia', after its
discoverer, who had slept a night on its gentle shore. Now it
was called simply Taupo, and at its northern end was a
thriving tourist resort that had taken its name. They passed
through the township, and left the rows of motels and hotels
along the foreshore to drive round the rim of the lake,
eventually arriving at the southern end and a smaller, quieter
settlement that nevertheless boasted a luxury hotel.

The lake was almost on the doorstep, and further south
was the high, snowy peak of Ruapehu. According to legend
the beautiful Ruapehu had once been married to the majestic
mountain, Taranaki, but was unfaithful to him with
Tongariro, another nearby volcano. After fighting
Tongariro, with much belching of fire and smoke and
flinging of enormous boulders, one of which fell into the lake
and became an island, Taranaki departed, grieving at his
wife's infidelity, and travelled to the west coast, his progress
carving a channel which filled with water and became the
Wanganui River. Ruapehu, repenting of her weakness,
rejected further advances from Tongariro, who ever since has
been smouldering with anger, rumbling and breathing fire.
Taranaki settled by the sea, and spent long years gazing
sorrowfully across the land at his errant wife from hundreds
of miles away.

Finding the story in one of the tourist pamphlets in the
hotel lobby, Trista was entranced, and when they drove out
to see Ruapehu and Tongariro on their high tussock plain
she looked at them with new eyes.

'They say that Taranaki will come back to her one day,'
she told Pierce. 'He's supposed to give a sign when he's
ready.'

'I should hope so,' Pierce said. 'We could do with a fair

warning. That would be something of an upheaval.'

'Would *you* come back?' she asked suddenly. 'If it happened to you?'

He looked at her consideringly. 'You're not planning to run off with a mountain, are you?'

She couldn't help laughing. But she said, 'You know what I mean.'

Brows lifted, he asked, 'What do you think?'

'You wouldn't, would you?' she said slowly. 'You might take a repentant wife back, but you'd never come to her.'

'I hope,' he said, 'we're talking theoretically here. May I remind you we're on our honeymoon?'

'I know,' she said, hooking her arms about his neck. 'Remind me again.'

His eyes kindled as he accepted the blatant invitation and kissed her eagerly parted mouth.

The night after their return home, she invited Geoffrey and Pierce's parents and Charley to dinner, serving trout that she and Pierce, under the expert supervision of a fisherman from the hotel, had caught in the lake. She had baked the two fish in foil with butter, herbs and white wine, having a little trouble fitting them into the oven. 'Their tails,' she told the guests, 'kept hanging over the dish and getting in the way.' However, the result was worth the trouble, they all assured her.

Pierce's family left first. As her mother and father were saying goodnight to Geoffrey and Trista, Charley plucked at Pierce's sleeve. 'Trista looks happy,' she murmured, causing him enormous amusement by the speculative, wondering glance she cast at him. 'Much more relaxed.'

'I'm sure that relieves your mind,' he said solemnly. 'What about me? Or doesn't my happiness matter?'

'Yes, of course it does! Only you're not . . . vulnerable, like Trista.'

'Fat lot *you* know, infant!' He tweaked her hair. His voice was bantering, but she looked at him searchingly, not sure if she imagined a slightly grim undercurrent.

After they had left, Geoffrey had already kissed Trista goodbye as Pierce stood beside her when he said, 'By the way, I've got word of my appointment to the Bench.'

'Congratulations,' Pierce said, shaking his hand.

Trista hugged her father. 'I'm very glad for you. I'm sure you deserve it.'

'Thank you. It'll mean changes in the firm—you'll need another partner to take some of the load, Pierce. I won't pretend I'm not pleased, though. I thought a small celebration dinner would be nice, quite soon. I'll want both of you there, of course.'

'I'll come round and help Mrs Kemp with the preparations,' Trista promised. 'Let us know the date.'

By the time Geoffrey's dinner party took place, the news was common knowledge, reported in a half-inch of type in the newspapers. There were twenty people around the table, including the partners and their wives, and the new partner, a young Maori woman with sleek dark hair smoothly drawn back from an oval face of classic beauty.

'She intimidates me,' Trista confessed to Pierce on their way home afterwards.

'Keita?' Pierce enquired. 'Don't be silly. She was actually scared stiff of the lot of us.'

'Scared?' Trista repeated disbelievingly. The young lawyer had looked the picture of poise and confidence, and she had a formidable intelligence that was obvious every time she opened her mouth.

'So she told me.'

'Is that why you spent so much time talking to her after dinner?' The two of them had spent half an hour on the sofa chatting together.

'Yes, actually. She's quite young, you know, to be offered a partnership in a firm like ours. Still feeling her way. It's all new to her.'

'Yes. Dad said you worked very hard to get the others to accept her. Why?'

'She's highly qualified, and it's time we had a woman in the firm. I'm sure she'll be an asset to us.'

'She's beautiful, too,' Trista said.

'Well, that can be an asset, as well. A bonus, I suppose.'

'You mean, you'd still have wanted her, even if she wasn't so nice to look at?'

'Yes.' He glanced down at her and said, 'Trista, you're not jealous, are you?'

Trista shook her head. 'What have I got to be jealous of?'

'Nothing. And surely you know that. You're not exactly a plain Jane yourself.'

'I told you, I'm not jealous!' And if she were, Trista thought, it wouldn't be of the other woman's looks. Pierce, as much as most men, liked women to look nice, but he admired women like Keita, like Glenda, women who had the drive and ambition to become lawyers and doctors. Or like his sisters. Antonia had been a dental nurse before she married, and Charley was forever talking about her work with the Water Board. Even his mother, a court stenographer before her marriage, had retrained and gone back to her profession when Charley was at college.

Trista had enjoyed her time at university, and her computer studies. She was willing to work and could imagine one day being interested enough to pursue a career, although she doubted if she would be as dedicated as either Glenda or Keita. But at the moment she had only one ambition, and that depended not so much on her own dedication to her goal as on the vagaries of nature.

Antonia's new baby was due after Christmas, but in November she was taken to hospital in premature labour, and the girl was born during that night.

'The baby's not well,' Pierce told Trista, giving her the news after talking to his mother on the telephone. 'It looks as though Toni will be in the hospital for some time. And of course all their plans for having the other two looked after are shot to pieces. Ken intended to take his holidays when Antonia was due. He and my mother are trying to arrange something else now.'

'We could take them,' Trista suggested. 'I'd love to look after them. You wouldn't mind, would you?'

'Of course I wouldn't mind. But two small children—do you think you could manage?'

Antonia had some doubts too, which she expressed to Pierce, rather than Trista, but Ken, relieved at the offer of help, told her not to fuss. 'The kids know Pierce and Trista, they'll enjoy having a little holiday. And I'm sure Trista can cope as well as anyone. She adores them both.'

Except for anxiety about Antonia and the new baby, Trista thoroughly enjoyed herself, although she found she was tired at the end of the day. Having two little ones in the house kept her continually busy, but she loved it. Antonia had written down detailed instructions as to the care and feeding of infants, and Trista soon established a routine similar to the one they were accustomed to at home. She got up before Pierce, and when he came in for breakfast he would find her supervising them while they ate their cereal, at the same time that she set a place for him. In the evenings she fed the children and put them to bed, sometimes prevailing upon him to read them a story while she tidied up the inevitable mess they made, and within the hour she would be placing dinner before him and sitting opposite looking fresh and groomed.

'I don't know how you do it,' he said once, and Trista blatently smirked.

'You expected me to be frazzled and bedraggled, your meals burnt and your washing not done,' she accused him.

'Not bedraggled,' he protested. 'But a bit harassed, perhaps.'

'Well, I'm not. Mind you, they're good kids. And Kirsten helps with her little brother. She's very sweet to him. And really looking forward to the new baby.'

'Antonia made a point of preparing her for Shane's arrival. I expect she's done the same this time.'

The children were allowed to visit their mother a couple of times, and peep through glass at the baby. On the way home, they peppered Trista with questions which she fielded deftly, and Pierce gave her a sideways glance of surprised respect.

'Did you ever think of working with children?' he asked her.

'No.'

Surprised at her abruptness, he looked askance.

'My father wanted me to be a teacher,' she said. 'But I didn't fancy it.'

'Not even kindergarten teaching?'

'No.' She changed the subject.

When at last the hospital said their little sister was well enough to go home with her mother, Trista was loath to let them go.

'You look quite bereft,' Pierce teased her, the day after they had delivered the children home. 'I've become used to seeing you with a child in your arms, or on your knee.'

'I've got used to it, too,' she said, adding wistfully, 'Do you think it will be long before we have one of our own?'

'It's early days yet,' Pierce advised her. 'I thought you might change your mind when you found out what it's really like, twenty-four hours a day.'

'I know you did. You still don't believe I know what I'm doing, do you?' she asked, with a hint of anger. 'Sometimes

I think you really don't want a family!'

'I've told you I do,' he said, drawing her into his arms. 'Give it time. We've hardly been married two months.'

Pierce suggested they give a party for the members of his firm before Christmas. Traditionally one of the partners entertained the rest at the end of the year, not just for the partners, but including the junior clerks and secretaries as well. 'And as I've recently acquired a new home and a new wife, I think they expect it to be me this year,' he told Trista.

She grimaced a little, but said, 'OK. With a buffet?'

'Can you manage it?'

'Of course.'

'You could get in some help, if you like.' He knew that, while she had played hostess for Geoffrey often enough, Mrs Kemp had done most of the cooking and serving.

'I'll manage,' Trista insisted, and he shrugged and said, 'Well, let me know if there's anything I can do.'

She prepared carefully, determined that the food should be quite superb, planning a menu that she could largely cook a day ahead and add the finishing touches to just before putting the dishes on the buffet-table.

The night before, she had the refrigerator stacked with mysterious bowls and dishes, and Pierce remarked appreciatively on the interesting smells in the kitchen.

'Don't touch!' she said sternly as he opened the door of the refrigerator. 'It's all for the party.' She had an apron about her waist, and was busy at the sink, washing up the last of the pots and dishes she had used, because the dishwasher was already full.

'What, all of it?' he asked plaintively.

'Don't touch!' she repeated. 'You've had dinner.'

Pierce sighed, closed the door and picked up a tea-towel,

coming to help her. 'You sound as though you're talking to Kirsten,' he said.

'Sorry'

He laughed, and leaned over to kiss her nape, where wisps of hair were escaping from the knot she had pinned up to keep it out of the way. 'Never mind.' He put down the bowl he was drying, and tossed the tea-towel on to the drying rack, shifting to stand behind her with his arms about her waist, his lips nuzzling at her nape again.

'Pierce!' she said breathlessly. 'I'm busy . . .'

'I'm hungry,' he growled. His teeth gently nipped her skin.

Trista placed a dripping wooden spoon on the rack. 'Pierce . . .' Helplessly, she leaned against him. 'I have to finish these . . .'

'I'll do them later,' he promised. His hand tugged at the knot of her apron, his lips now on the curve of her neck and shoulder.

The apron joined the tea-towel. His hand homed on her breast.

'You can't get round me that way,' she said, weakly.

She felt the small laugh that shook him. 'Can't I?' he asked confidently, and turned her in his arms.

Her hands left the sink and dripped water on the floor. 'Pierce!' she wailed. But there was laughter in her eyes, on her lips. He tipped her back over his arm, and she said, 'You are not getting anything to eat!'

'If you're sending me to bed without any supper,' he said, 'you're coming, too!' His mouth was skimming her throat now, and she gave a gurgle of laughter that turned to a gasp of pleasure.

He pulled her upright against him, and she said, 'There's bread and cheese . . .'

'I'm not a mouse,' he said. 'Didn't we decide that once before?'

She made to bring her hands to his chest, and realised that they were still covered with soapy water. 'I'm dripping!' she said.

He laughed again. 'I just said, I'm not a mouse. But I could eat *you*, all the same.'

'You fool!' Trista laughed too. 'You know what I mean. My hands are all wet.'

'Never mind,' he said, taking her head between his palms, his eyes alight with laughing desire. 'Stop fussing, Trista, and kiss me.'

When his mouth came down on hers, she lifted her hands, held them in the air for a few seconds, then, as her body curved instinctively to his, put her arms about him and flattened her wet palms on his back. She felt him shiver, and trembled in turn. As his lips moved over hers, she mumbled, 'I thought you were hungry.'

'I am,' he said. 'Can't you tell?' And he hauled her closer.

Her laughter was smothered by his mouth as he deepened the kiss. Then he swung her off her feet and carried her into their bedroom.

The next day she went into town to buy some fresh ingredients for garnishes and salads. She also saw displayed in a shop window a dress that she couldn't resist, a pretty, full-skirted dress made of hot pink silk. When she tried it and found that it fitted like a dream, she wrote out a cheque and bore it triumphantly out of the shop. She would look great tonight, and the dinner would be the best. Pierce would be proud of her. The cheque had made a hole in their bank account, though. Pierce had asked her if she wanted her own account, or a joint one with him, and she had opted for a joint one. The money, after all, came from his earnings. He never commented on what she spent, but she looked at the row of figures and felt a twinge of unease. Perhaps she should have asked him first . . .

She was piling bags into her car when she was hailed by a friend whom she hadn't seen since her wedding.

'You look *well*!' the girl said.

Trista laughed and answered, 'Don't sound so surprised.'

'Oh, well . . . we were all surprised at you getting married—but how's that yummy husband of yours? Listen, what about lunch—a drink, anyway? We never see each other these days. Haven't dumped your old friends, have you, now that you're married?'

Sally had always talked too much, and she wasn't renowned for tact. Trista said, 'Of course I haven't. I've just been busy, that's all. Getting the house fixed up and all that.'

Sally looked sceptical, and Trista began to feel a little guilty. She had not kept in touch with her friends. The crowd she used to go about with seemed pretty juvenile these days. And anyway, Pierce filled her life . . .

She agreed to lunch, at a bistro bar not far from Pierce's office near the courthouse. So it shouldn't have been too surprising that Pierce himself walked in as they were starting on their meal. But Trista couldn't help the small, unpleasant sense of shock that came with the realisation that he had a woman with him.

A moment later, she recognised Keita, the new partner in his office. A group of businessmen leaving the bistro almost bumped into them, and as Keita stepped swiftly aside Pierce's hand came up to her waist, steadying her. Keita turned her head and smiled and said something to him before she stepped away and they went towards a table in the corner. A table for two, Trista noted, ignoring the fact that the place was almost full, and that, apart from the one littered with dirty glasses and plates that the businessmen had just left, there was very little choice.

Sally was chattering, but she didn't hear a word. She knew she should wave to Pierce, call, tell Sally casually, 'Oh, there's my husband, shall we ask him and his partner to join us?' She did none of those things. She hunched down in her high-backed seat, turned half away from the room, and watched morbidly, covertly, as Pierce got drinks for himself and his companion, ordered a meal, sat talking to Keita over the small table. Keita wasn't smiling now, as she sipped at her drink and picked at the food before her, and Pierce leaned over the table towards her. The conversation looked very . . . intimate.

Don't be a fool, Trista told herself. They're partners, they probably have a lot to talk about. It's business. Then she saw Keita duck her head and raise a hand to her eyes, brushing first one and then the other, wiping away tears.

Her other hand lay on the table, and Trista sat riveted as Pierce put his over it. Something cold closed about her heart and squeezed as she watched her husband, sitting there holding another woman's hand.

CHAPTER TEN

'PUDDING?' asked Sally, and as Trista wrenched away her eyes and stared at her vacantly, 'Sweets?'

'Oh. No, not for me,' Trista said. But if they got up and left now Pierce would see them. 'Coffee,' she said. 'But . . . not yet. I'd like to wait a while, talk . . . We haven't seen each other for such ages.'

That was no hardship for Sally. Trista tried to concentrate, to answer with some semblance of intelligence. It was a nightmare. It wasn't true. She was imagining things. She was, there was a perfectly simple explanation.

Pierce went out with his arm about Keita's shoulder. Mercifully, Sally had sat with her back to them the whole time. There *must* be an explanation, of course there was . . .

'Coffee,' she said, cutting Sally off in mid-sentence. 'I'm ready for some now, are you?'

She got home and went on with the preparations she had planned, automatically, her mind in neutral. Except that every now and then it ran riot, inventing possible and impossible scenarios . . . Keita and Pierce were lovers, perhaps had been for a long time. That was why he had been so keen for her to be the new partner. Or, when Keita had joined the firm, he had realised that this was the kind of woman he should have married, someone who was his

124

equal, who could understand his job, work beside him, as Trista could never do. She read about his court cases sometimes in the paper, but he never discussed them with her, never told her what he was working on. Keita could share that with him, help him.

He didn't love Trista, he had never pretended to, never said so. Even last night—and her stomach curled at the memory of last night, of their lovemaking—he had not said he loved her. He never did. Never would. Had he said it to Keita?

Her rational mind said, Pierce would never be unfaithful. Never. Even if . . .

And then the dreadful fantasies took over again. He would be faithful to her, but at what price? Tied to her, and longing for another woman . . . could she do that to him? But could she bear to let him go?

I'll fight, she thought grimly, stripping the outer leaves from a lettuce. I'll fight for him. And her mind jeered, You selfish bitch . . . he wants her, not you; let him go. She gave the base of the lettuce a vicious twist, breaking it off, and turned the tap on full blast to wash the remaining leaves.

'He doesn't want to go,' she muttered, banging a bowl down on the table. 'He married me—he knew what he was doing. He had his reasons—even if they didn't include loving me. He can't change his mind now. I won't let him.'

Absently her fingers tore at the crisp leaves. But how could I bear to have him stay, if he loves someone else?

Don't be silly, said her rational self. How could he make love to you as he does if he was thinking of another woman?

But perhaps he could, just *because* he was thinking of Keita, imagining Keita in his arms . . .

It didn't help that Pierce was late, coming in with apologies for not being home sooner, offering help which she construed as the result of a guilty conscience.

'It's all done,' she said, determined not to show her feelings, for some reason feeling it was more important than ever that this evening should go off without a hitch. Which meant, among other things, that of course they couldn't have a flaming row just before the guests arrived. 'Everything's ready,' she told him. 'I just have to get dressed and then spend a few minutes in the kitchen before everyone gets here. Do you mind if I have the shower before you?'

'Feel free,' he said. 'You're not nervous about tonight, are you?'

'Nervous?' Trista managed a rather artificial laugh. 'Of course not.' She disappeared into the shower.

When she came out and he saw her dress, he pursed his lips admiringly, saying, 'That's new, isn't it?'

Bridling a little, she said, 'Yes. I thought you'd want me to look good tonight.'

A little surprised, he said, 'You always look good, Trista. It's very nice.'

Lifting her chin, she said, 'It . . . cost rather a lot.'

'Did it, indeed? Well, as long as we're not in overdraft over it . . .'

She shook her head. 'Of course not. I wouldn't do that.'

He knotted his tie and came over to her. 'I know you wouldn't,' he said, and made to kiss her, but she evaded him.

'I've just put on my make-up.'

'Sorry.' He moved away from her. 'Anyway, you look lovely.'

'Thank you.'

He looked askance at the formality of her tone, a faint frown appearing between his brows. He touched her arm lightly. 'It's going to be a great party,' he assured her.

He thought she was nervous, in spite of her denials. She wasn't, but she was keyed up, tense, on her mettle. Tonight she was competing.

She was dazzling. She knew how to be, and pulled out all the stops. All the men fell over themselves to be near her. Except Pierce, who greeted Keita with a kiss on her smooth golden-olive cheek, and softness in his eyes. Trista kissed her too, feeling like Judas, and led her into the party, making her welcome, smiling at her, hating her.

Once or twice, Trista realised that Pierce was observing her rather narrowly, the smile on his face a little twisted. Her father wore an expression of faint trepidation.

Pierce had told her the pattern of the office parties. Drinks and food, and conversation to discreet background music, until about eleven, when the guests would start to drift off, except for a few diehards who might stick it out until midnight. But at ten-thirty Trista put a rock record on the CD player and invited one of the younger men to dance with her. He grinned hugely, excused himself to the girl he had brought with him, and accepted the invitation with alacrity. From then on the party began to swing. Several of the men shifted furniture out of the way under Trista's direction to make space, and dancing became fairly general. Geoffrey and the older couples had left by midnight, as expected, Geoffrey with a frowning look at his daugther as she gaily bade him goodnight, but the younger ones were just getting into the mood, and they didn't depart until several hours later, declaring with obvious but enthusiastic surprise that they'd had a fantastic time.

'There's certainly never been an office party like it,' Pierce admitted, as he closed the door after them.'

'It was good, wasn't it?' Trista said brightly, and turned from him to start clearing up the debris.

'They certainly thought so.' He followed her, watching as she efficiently gathered up a tray full of used plates and glasses. 'Why not leave that till morning?'

'It *is* morning.'

'You know what I mean. I'll help you clean it all up tomorrow.'

He walked over to take the tray from her hands, but she clung stubbornly to it. 'No, I'll do it now.'

'It will take hours.'

She shrugged. 'So . . . it'll take hours.'

He stared at her. 'OK. We'll do it now.'

'I don't need your help.'

She had meant to sound offhand, but it came out sharp.

'What's the matter?' he asked quietly, stepping back.

'Nothing. There's no need for you to stay up, simply because I'd rather do this now. Go to bed, if you like.'

But instead he followed her into the kitchen, and as soon as she had put down the tray on the table, took her arm and swung her about to face him.

Trista pulled away violently, coming up against the table behind her.

Pierce's brows drew together, his eyes going hard as he directed a cold, questioning stare at her. She thought he might look like that in court, and her heart gave a tiny thump of fright.

'What is going on, Trista?' he asked her. His voice was quiet but implacable.

'Nothing.' She made to turn away from him in the direction of the sink, but he caught at her wrists, capturing them both in a firm, unbreakable grip.

'Come on,' he said. 'Come clean. What's happened to upset you?'

Looking at him blindly, she said, 'I'm not upset——'

Pierce gave her a little shake. 'Don't tell me lies,' he said.

'What about *you?*' she shot back at him then.

'Me?' he said blankly. '*What* about me? What are you talking about?'

She bit her lip. 'Have you never told me lies?' she challenged him. He still had that almost frightening look in his eyes. She repeated huskily, 'Have you never told me lies?'

He was silent for a moment before he said, 'In what connection, exactly?'

'*Any* connection!' she cried wildly. 'Have you?'

'No,' he said tersely. 'I don't tell lies, Trista. Now, will you for pete's sake tell me what this is all about?'

'I saw you,' she said sulkily. 'Today. At lunch.'

His expression didn't alter by one iota. 'So?'

'I bumped into Sally,' she explained. 'Sally Cremorne—she was at our wedding . . .'

Impatiently, he repeated. '*So?*'

'We . . . had lunch at that bistro, near your office.'

'So did I,' he said. 'I didn't see you.'

'I know. You were with Keita.'

He said in a level voice, 'I know who I had lunch with, thanks.' His hands had tightened on her wrists. For the third time, he said, 'So?'

Trista looked down at their hands. Her shoulders lifted in a small, hopeless shrug. 'You . . . were holding her hand.'

She saw his chest rise and fall. His grip shifted from her wrists to her shoulders. He rocked her back and forth chidingly. 'Trista, Trista!' he said. 'You incredible little idiot! Why didn't you just come over and say hello?'

Her eyes sparkling with tears of chagrin, she said, 'How could I? You seemed to be . . .'

His voice suddenly stern, he said, 'What?' And when she didn't answer, he said, 'Go on. We seemed to be . . .?'

'I thought you wanted to be alone,' she muttered evasively. Then, looking up she added resentfully, 'You *were* holding her hand!'

His mouth a little grim, he agreed. 'Yes, I was. And on the strength of that, you concluded I was having a torrid affair with our junior partner, is that it?' His hands tightened again. 'I'm not sure I oughtn't to spank you!' he said. 'I think I'm insulted.'

She looked up at him hopefully. 'Well . . . what *were* you doing?'

'Having lunch,' he replied tantalisingly.

Trista's eyes sparked with temper, and he added, 'Taking Keita out to lunch in the hope of helping her get over a stressful time. We'd been in court all morning. She was assisting me in a child abuse case. She'd been fine with the paperwork, very professional, very objective, reading all the nasty details. But in court we were confronted with the victim. She hadn't had to face that before. She was OK in there, but afterwards she let go a bit. I thought it would do her good to have a drink and a decent meal, in the company of someone who'd been through it and could understand what she was feeling.'

'You're defending the abuser?'

'The alleged abuser. He's entitled to a fair trial, no matter what he's accused of. It's my job to see he gets, it.'

'I know.' Her father had explained all that, when she was a young teenager and full of indignant idealism.

'But Keita,' Pierce explained, 'was having her first crisis of that sort—it's something every young barrister must face, sooner or later.'

'So you . . . comforted her.'

'Yes.'

'And . . . that's all it was?' Her eyes searched his anxiously.

'For goodness' sake, Trista!' he said in a goaded voice. 'I shouldn't have to tell you that!' He suddenly hauled her close and covered her mouth with an angry, exasperated kiss, hard and passionate.

For a moment she remained rigid in his arms, then hers wound about him, and she returned the kiss fiercely, with an overwhelming relief.

'You little *fool*!' he groaned against her neck, holding her close. 'What on earth gave you the idea that I'd think of any other woman when I've got you . . .?'

'I'm sorry, I'm sorry!' she whispered, her lips feverishly touching his cheek, his eyebrow, the corner of his mouth.

'I should think so!' His arms tightened until they endangered her ability to breathe. 'I'll make you sorry, all right.'

She gave a breathless little squeal as he lifted her into his arms.

'Shut up!' he said masterfully.

Trista laughed, and he grinned back at her, then strode

along the passage, pushed the door of the bedroom shut with his foot and threw her on to the softness of the bed.

'What are you going to do?' she asked in mock fear.

'Guess.' He dropped his tie to the carpet and began unbuttoning his shirt.

Demurely, she said, 'I can't think.'

Casting off the shirt, he sat on the bed and began taking off his shoes. 'Can't you?' he asked. 'Use your imagination.'

Trista shut her eyes tightly. 'Oooh!'

She heard his soft laughter before he slid on to the bed beside her.

'I'm going to ravish you,' he said. And proceeded to do so.'

On Christmas Day they had lunch at Pierce's parents' house with the rest of the family. Ken's mother was there, too, and Mrs Allyn had invited Geoffrey, but he declined. Hester would have dinner at his house, and Pierce and Trista were invited to join them.

When Trista, panting and smiling from a game of chase with the children, picked up some plates from the table where they had eaten outdoors and took them into the kitchen to help her mother-in-law, Mrs Allyn said quietly, 'Shouldn't you be taking it easy, dear?'

Surprised, Trista coloured. 'I'm all right.'

'You look blooming,' Pierce's mother assured her. 'I'm not surprised my son can't keep his eyes off you. But you're pregnant, aren't you?'

'I'm not sure yet,' Trista said. 'I hope so . . . how did you know?'

Mrs Allyn chuckled. 'I'm surprised everyone hasn't twigged. Some women get a special glow about them. To me, it's perfectly obvious. Have you said anything to Pierce?'

Trista shook her head. A little nervously she added, 'Do you think he'll be pleased?'

'My dear, he'll be delighted!' Mrs Allyn hugged her. 'Now you sit down in the sun for a while. I can manage here, and I see Charley's on her way to help anyway. Go and see a doctor after the holiday, and I'm sure you'll find I'm right.'

'I haven't been feeling sick, or anything,' Trista told Glenda doubtfully, when she visited her in her surgery. 'Shouldn't I be, by now?'

'Don't ask for it!' Glenda advised her crisply. 'Some people are lucky, and maybe you're one of them. You have all the physical signs, and the test confirms them. You can tell Pierce tonight that he's going to be a father. I only wish I could be there.' She laughed. 'No, I don't mean that. I'm pleased for you both. I know you want this baby very much.' Her face softened. 'The medical history you've given me, and my examination, gives me no reason to expect any problems. Of course, I can't make any promises . . . sometimes things go wrong for no foreseeable reason. Don't do anything extra-strenuous that's not been in your normal routine, but don't coddle yourself unduly, and you should have a lovely healthy baby in a bit over seven months' time.'

'You won't say anything to Pierce, will you?'

'My dear girl, what goes on in this room is strictly between you and your doctor—and I want to thank you for trusting me with that role, by the way. No, telling Pierce anything at all would be more than my career is worth. That's entirely a matter for you and your husband.'

'Yes. I'm sorry. You see, I . . .'

'It's all right, Trista. I understand. You'll be a lovely mother—and Pierce will be a super father. This is going to be one very lucky baby.'

'Well, it didn't take long,' Pierce said, 'to get what you wanted. Your father warned me.'

Trista looked up quickly, but he was smiling. 'You are pleased, aren't you?'

'Yes, I am pleased. It takes some getting used to, though, the idea of being a father. I did wonder about that smug little smile you've been wearing lately . . . Are you allowed a drink to celebrate?'

'Glenda said a very small one probably wouldn't do any harm . . . but I think I'd rather be on the safe side and stick to fruit juice.'

'One fruit juice coming up,' he promised.

When they had toasted the news, Pierce said, 'About other things . . . I suppose you must be careful?'

Trista looked at him sideways. 'Isn't it a bit late for that?'

He laughed. 'You know what I mean.'

Of course she did. And suddenly she wanted very much to make love to him, to have him love her. 'Oh, that!' she said with apparent carelessness. 'Glenda said it's OK . . .' She leaned close to him on the sofa and began playing with his shirt buttons, peeping at him from under her lashes. 'Just as long as I'm gentle with you . . .'

He laughed again, and she pressed her lips against the pulse in his throat. He caught at her hair and raised her face, finding her mouth. Her bones were turning to warm treacle. She closed her eyes, recognising a new tenderness in his handling of her. Tonight, she thought . . . tonight he might say the words he had never said to her. Always, he told her she was lovely, stunning, fantastic, a wonder. He admired her skin, her hair, the shape of her legs, her breasts. He told her that he wanted her, that he could make love to her endlessly, forever. But he had never told her that he loved her.

And tonight, after all, was no different. He was gentle, and passionate, and drew her with him into a world where nothing existed but the most exquisite pleasure she had known, centred on his mouth, his hands, his body. But when it was over, and she floated slowly down from the heights, locked securely in his arms, her cheek against his chest, something deep inside remained unsatisfied, hankering for the unattainable. 'You're so beautiful,' he had said. 'You're incredible. I love doing this to you, the way you respond . . .' But he had not said, I love you.

Pierce's family greeted the news with unequivocal pleasure. Geoffrey, strangely, seemed rather put out by it. 'I thought you might have waited a bit,' he told Pierce when they were alone.

'I'd have been content to wait,' Pierce said. 'But you told me yourself that Trista can be determined. And it was what she wanted. She's over the moon.'

'Yes,' Geoffrey said. 'I dare say she is.'

'She thought you'd be delighted.'

'Well . . . a grandson would be nice,' Geoffrey admitted gruffly.

'Would you settle for a granddaughter?' Pierce asked. 'I'm afraid we can't guarantee the sex.'

Geoffrey gave him a feeble smile. 'Either, of course,' he conceded. 'So long as Trista's happy.'

Pierce laughed. 'As I said, happy scarcely describes

it. She isn't even suffering from morning sickness yet.'

As it happened, she hardly ever did. Everything seemed to be going even better than Glenda had expected, and Trista threw herself into preparations, haunting babywear shops and installing nursery furniture in the room earmarked for the expected new arrival.

Pierce teased, 'You seem to live in this room. Every time I come home you're mooning in here.'

'I'm not mooning—I'm planning. And your dinner's in the oven.'

'I'm not bothered about my dinner. How about dinner out tomorrow? There won't be the same opportunity for that sort of thing, once the baby arrives.'

'Yes, OK,' she replied absently, smoothing the crib cover she had bought the day before. 'If you like.'

'With all this absorption in the baby,' he teased, 'I'm in danger of feeling left out. Isn't that one of the things that they warn you new mothers about?'

'You wouldn't be jealous!' she scoffed, then with less certainty added, 'Would you?'

'What do you think?'

'You're far too adult for that.'

'Still, I'll take you out tomorrow night, while we still have the chance. You might miss the social life later,' he warned, putting an arm about her shoulders.

Trista made a face at him. 'You're a regular Cassandra,' she told him a little crossly. 'How can I convince you that this is what I *want*—you, a home, our baby . . .?'

'It sounds very cosy,' he said.

Trista pushed away from him. 'Why say it like that?'

'Like what?' he asked carefully.

'In that yes-dear-*but* sort of voice. As though you don't

really believe that I can be serious about it. For heaven's sake, Pierce, I'm not just playing house!'

That was so close to what he sometimes suspected that he looked, for a moment, discomfited.

Trista saw it, and stalked out of the room. When he came into the kitchen she was banging the oven door decisively, and contrived to be so busy with pots and spoons and various utensils that she drove him to the lounge, where he sat reading the paper and wincing at the various thumps, slams and thuds emanating from the other room.

Dinner was delicious, but it was an uncomfortable meal. Trista asked with freezing politeness after his day, and when his lips twitched, her eyes sparkled with temper.

'It was very productive, thank you,' Pierce answered her question.

'What are you doing?'

'I've pretty well wrapped up a case that will be in court next week.'

He didn't expand on that, and Trista said, 'You can talk to me about your work, you know. I'm a barrister's daughter, after all.'

'You don't have to take an interest in my work, to keep me from having my nose put out of joint by the baby,' Pierce said drily. 'I was teasing.'

Stiffly, she said, 'I wasn't. Does it ever occur to you that I might have an intelligent interest in grown-up topics?'

Pierce's breath hissed between his teeth. 'Has it occurred to *you* that I would rather leave my work at the office and in the courtroom, where it belongs, and come home to something . . . different? Frankly, I get enough adversarial combat in court without having to face it here, too.'

Trista's face flamed. 'I'm sorry,' she said, and jumped up, leaving the table.

Pierce caught her before she reached the door, and hauled her into his arms. She pushed against him, but he didn't let go. 'No, *I'm* sorry,' he said. 'I shouldn't have snapped at you, and you in a delicate condition, too.'

She gave a small, reluctant snort of laughter. 'Glenda says I'm as fit as a fiddle.' She rested against him. 'Is that your courtroom manner?'

'Something like it, perhaps. If you're really interested, why don't you come and watch some time?'

She looked at him suspiciously, wondering if she was being offered a sop.

'Not anything too sordid and gory,' Pierce suggested. 'Especially while you're pregnant. But some cases aren't so bad. This one next week, for instance.'

'Would you like me to?' she asked.

'Only if you feel you want to.'

'All right. Perhaps I will.' She had seen her father in court a couple of times while she was still at school. He had been impressive, a figure of authority. Pierce's style, she was sure, would be different.

She did go and watch, sitting in the public gallery and finding that her husband had turned into a tall, very formal stranger in his wig and gown. The case was one of burglary and assault, and the accused pleaded mistaken identity. Trista watched Pierce cross-examining the witness, his manner polite but incisive. When the accused was found not guilty, she almost applauded.

'I always knew you'd be a demon in court,' she told him that night after they had gone to bed.

He laughed. 'Rubbish. I'm just a lawyer doing my job.'

'You do it awfully well. I've seen my father in action a couple of times, and you're at least as good as he is. Do you want to be a judge some day?'

'First things first,' he said. 'Queen's Counsel will do for starters.'

'Yes. When?'

He laughed. 'When it comes. Your father says he's already putting in a good word in the right quarters. But in the end, it's up to me. I have to prove myself so good that other lawyers will be willing to come and ask me to represent their clients.'

'You are that good.'

'Well, thanks for the vote of confidence.' He had his arm about her, her head cradled against his shoulder. 'How are you feeling?'

'I'm fine. I feel wonderful.'

'Honestly?'

'Honestly. Glenda's pleased with me.'

She certainly seemed remarkably well—'positively incandescent,' Charley said, almost enviously. Charley, almost as thrilled as Trista herself about the baby, had been shopping with her for baby clothes, and complained that Trista in a delicate condition had more energy than her sister-in-law in the peak of health and definitely unpregnant. Everyone remarked on how blooming Trista looked, and Glenda said with a chuckle that she was waiting for petals to appear at any moment.

So it was a thunderous shock to Pierce when he came home one day to find Trista lying on the sofa, white-faced and tight-lipped with pain.

'Call Glenda,' she gasped, as he knelt at her side, filled with sudden, terrified concern. 'Get Glenda. I think I'm losing the baby.'

CHAPTER ELEVEN

GLENDA got her into hospital, but even specialist care couldn't save the baby.

'Just one of those things,' Glenda told Pierce sadly. 'We don't know why. Sometimes it's nature's way of discarding a foetus that's less than perfect. Contrary to popular belief, it's actually quite hard to dislodge a healthy baby from the womb. This may be for the best . . . but that's not a lot of comfort to Trista just now.'

'No.' He closed his eyes, remembering Trista's face when he held her hand while Glenda told her the baby was gone. The frozen, hopeless look of despair that had not lifted since. 'You know,' he confessed, 'I've been almost jealous of that baby. Now . . . I'd do anything to give it back to her.'

'There's no reason why there can't be others,' Glenda said. 'There shouldn't be any damage, and she could get pregnant again quite soon. Some women want to try again immediately, if they've lost a child, whether before birth or afterwards.'

'Surely we should wait a little, after this?'

'I'd prefer it, from the point of view of her physical health. But she's badly knocked, emotionally, and if that would help her . . . maybe. A miscarriage can shake a woman's confidence, you know, make her feel terribly inadequate, although in Trista's case . . . Well, as I said, some people seem to need to fill the gap the child has left in

their lives as soon as possible. We have unmarried girls
presenting themselves pregnant again less than a year after
giving up their first baby, or even after having a
termination. It isn't because they're promiscuous. It's a
very powerful natural instinct. Perhaps you should be
guided by her feelings.'

'I did that before,' Pierce said rather harshly, 'and this
happened!'

'That isn't very rational,' Glenda said gently.

'I don't feel rational. I feel . . .'

'Angry,' Glenda supplied. 'I know—it's unfair; she didn't
deserve it; why her, when so many people who don't want
babies have them so easily?'

'You know it all?' Pierce asked wryly.

'I've seen people go through it before. It's natural to be
angry. I would be. I *am*. But anger won't help Trista.'

Nothing seemed to help. Trista came home, glanced at the
closed door of the room so hopefully decorated and
furnished, and walked right past it. She responded with
pathetic politeness when Pierce—or anyone—spoke to her,
and kept the house almost uncannily neat and clean. Six
weeks after the miscarriage, he took her to Glenda's surgery
and sat in the waiting-room while Trista had her
examination.

'Everything's fine,' she said listlessly afterwards. 'Glenda
said there's nothing to be concerned about.' Pierce cast her
a worried glance and decided to speak to Glenda himself,
later.

'I could give her anti-depressants,' Glenda told him, 'but
it isn't always a good idea. Grieving is a process that needs
going through. I know it's painful to watch, but
suppressing it may do more harm than good. Be patient,

and give her all the support and loving care that you can.'

He was, and he did, and nothing changed. He lived with a ghost. 'It's as though all the lights have been turned out,' he told his mother, 'inside her.' He didn't know what to do. If he put his arms about her she allowed it, but he didn't feel she derived any comfort from the gesture. When he kissed her, her skin was cool and pale. She seemed to have forgotten how to smile. Sometimes she looked almost plain.

Geoffrey called several times, and she presented her cheek dutifully to him and looked straight through him when he talked to her. Charley visited for a weekend, and left with tears in her eyes. Hester carried her off to a show and returned her, saying, 'I'm afraid she isn't ready yet, Pierce. I don't think she took in any of it.'

His own mother said, 'Don't worry, it can't last forever. The poor child just didn't think anything could go wrong, I suppose. What about taking her to see Antonia? She's so fond of little Kirsten. That might bring her out of it.'

But when he suggested it Trista cried, 'No!' Almost fearfully, she added, 'Please, no! Not yet.'

'All right,' he said. 'We don't have to. We'll wait until you feel up to it.'

One night, remembering the headlong passion she had so eagerly shared, he deliberately set out to seduce her, hoping that might break through the icy wall that surrounded her. She accepted his kisses, his embrace, even put her arms about his neck, and obediently opened herself to his body. But it obviously did nothing for her, and when he rolled away, his arm flung over his eyes, she said in a quiet little voice into the darkness, 'I'm sorry.'

'No,' he said, finding her hand and holding it tightly. 'It isn't your fault. It doesn't matter. I thought it might help.'

'Oh.'

For a moment he was shaken by swift, hot anger. 'For heaven's *sake*!' he said. 'Do you think I'd force myself on you for my own selfish pleasure?'

'No,' she answered remotely. 'You're not like that. You've always been very kind to me.'

As if he were some stranger who had rendered her some impersonal service. Pierce closed his eyes against a strong urge to weep. 'Oh, Trista . . . I didn't mean to yell.'

'That's all right. I suppose it's understandable.' She added, 'I am trying.'

'I know,' he said. 'I know.' It was the trying that was so damned heartbreaking.

Geoffrey decided at last to take the bull by the horns. He invited himself to lunch one Sunday, and Trista cooked a roast and vegetables. Her cooking these days was uninspired, if competent. It was a long time since Pierce had come home to find her arranging artichoke hearts on a plate with artistic garnishes, or anxiously stirring butter into some new kind of sauce.

'Now then,' Geoffrey said, as they sat in the lounge with their coffee. He cleared his throat, and Pierce, alert to Geoffrey's mannerisms by now, looked up at him quickly.

'Trista!' her father said imperatively, dragging her attention to himself. 'We all know you've been through a difficult time,' he continued with clumsy compassion. 'But you can't keep moping forever, you know. It's time you snapped out of it. Pierce has been very patient with you, but you're not being fair to him. After all, it was his baby too, remember.'

For an instant her stricken gaze lit on his face. Pierce opened his mouth to protest, then shut it firmly. Nobody else had got through to her. Geoffrey was her father. He knew her, presumably, better than any of them.

She was staring down at her hands now, curled listlessly about her half-empty cup. Geoffrey ploughed on. 'It's gone on long enough. Naturally you're disappointed—we're all disappointed—my first grandchild, you know.'

Trista looked up at him then, and Pierce stiffened, a sudden line appearing between his brows. The dull apathy he had become accustomed to seeing in her eyes had given way to a searing hostility.

If Geoffrey noticed, he refused to back down. 'But,' he said, 'you're young and healthy, and there's no reason why you can't have a perfectly healthy baby next time. The doctors have told you that.'

'There was no reason this time,' she said. 'None. They can't explain it. It just happened,' she added bitterly. 'And it could happen again.'

'You mustn't think like that.'

Suddenly blazing, Trista said, between clenched teeth, *'One thing you can't do is tell me how to think!'*

Taken aback, Geoffrey said angrily, 'Now then, young lady——'

'You've told me what to do all my *life*—and I've done it,' Trista cried bitterly. 'But what I think, and what I *feel*—that's *my* business. *That* you can't control!'

'Whatever I've done has always been for your own good, you know that.'

'Do I?' she shot back at him, her eyes wide and clear. 'That's what you've always told me. You were so sure that you knew what was good for me.'

'Well, of course! I'm your father——'

Trista leapt to her feet, still clutching her cup in both hands. 'Didn't it ever occur to you that you might be *wrong?'*

Geoffrey shot a glance at Pierce, tense and alert in his chair. 'Look,' he said uncomfortably, 'I know what you mean, my dear. It's no use dwelling on what's past.'

'Yes, you know what I mean,' Trista retorted. 'But you have no idea how I feel. You never have.'

'That's quite unfair!' Geoffrey got to his feet too.

'Unfair? Oh, I'm *sorry*!' Trista said sarcastically. 'Have you any idea how I feel *now*?' she demanded. 'I feel guilty. I feel as though I'm being punished. As though I don't deserve to have a healthy baby, because I've already had my chance. And that there'll never be another . . . not for me. And I feel as though I've cheated my husband, because he wants a family too, and it's my fault if we can't have one. *That's* how I feel now.'

'But that's ridiculous!'

Trista raised her eyes to the ceiling, then squeezed them shut. Her voice husky with emotion, she said, 'Ridiculous or not, it's how I *feel*!' Looking at him again, she added almost wearily, 'But my feelings have never been very important to you.'

'That's not true!' Geoffrey flushed indignantly. 'You're just being a silly little adolescent again, full of self-pity and blaming everyone for your troubles. Well, it's not good enough any more. You've got to put all that behind you, Trista, and grow up!'

Something in Trista snapped. Pierce saw the lift of her head, the angry spark in her eyes, before her hands moved, one dropping to her side, the other sweeping back and forward with the cup in it, flinging the cold coffee at her father's expensive tweed jacket and co-ordinated shirt and tie.

'How dare you?' she shouted at him as Geoffrey gaped at her, the coffee making dark wet stains on his clothes, and

dripping down on to his shoes. He flinched as she drew her
arm back again, but the cup went sailing harmlessly into the
fireplace, where it smashed loudly against the iron grate.
Pierce was on his feet, his eyes riveted on Trista's flushed,
furious face.

'You *dare* talk to me about growing up?' she cried,
apparently oblivious to Pierce's presence, her eyes wide and
fierce. 'I grew up when I was barely seventeen! When you
took my baby away from me!'

'I didn't——'

'Yes. You made me give her up—I never wanted to, you
knew I wanted to keep her. But I couldn't stand out against
you, not after Chris . . . If only he'd . . .'

Geoffrey had taken out a handkerchief and was
ineffectually trying to wipe himself down, in between
casting offended, harassed glances at his daughter.

Pierce, stunned by the implication of what they were
saying, saw the tears gather in Trista's eyes. Her mouth
trembled. '"You'll forget it," you told me. "Put it all
behind you, and everything will be just the way it was. *I
know what's best for you!*" Well, you didn't know, and I
didn't forget it—not ever, not for a moment! I had a baby,
and she's gone forever, and it's your fault! *I hate you for it!*'

Geoffrey stepped towards her, his hand outstretched.
'Now, Trista! That's nonsense.'

'*Don't come near me!*' she said sharply. 'Don't.'

'Sit down——' Geoffrey urged, grabbing her arm.

It was like a match to tinder. She hit out at him, her fists
connecting with his arm, his chest, his face, her breath fast,
sobbing.

Taken aback, Geoffrey lifted his arms to defend himself
from the attack. Pierce lunged forward and caught a flailing
wrist, pulling her away and into his arms. She fought him

for about a minute, but he held her tightly, closely, until her resistance died. 'No,' he said. 'No, darling. It's all right. Stop now. It's all right.'

Her body shaken by tearing sobs, she at last subsided against him, and over her head he said to Geoffrey, 'You'd better go.'

'She's hysterical. Shall I get something . . . water?'

'Just go.'

'I don't like leaving her like this . . . Trista!' he said loudly. 'Pull yourself together!'

Pierce said, 'Geoffrey, please just go!'

'She's always been highly strung, but it's no good giving in to her, you know . . .'

Pierce's temper broke its bounds. 'For heaven's sake, Geoffrey, *get out*!'

Geoffrey's face took on a thunderous expression. He nodded stiffly and left, closing the front door ostentatiously behind him. Pierce stood with his wife in his arms, his hand stroking her hair, while she cried as though she would never stop.

When at last the shuddering sobs eased, she moved away from his hold and took the handkerchief he handed her without looking at him. 'Thank you,' she said, her voice husky. 'I'll go to the bedroom, if you don't mind. I'd . . . like to be alone for a while.'

When she had gone, he stood where she had left him. He felt as though someone had hit him over the head with a blunt object. All his thinking about Trista and their relationship had to be rearranged. Nothing was what it had seemed. A whole lot of puzzling pieces of knowledge about her fell into place. Even his own feelings had changed in some strange, subtle ways. He was groping in the dark, confused and angry, and he was aware that the anger, at least, had to be contained and controlled before he faced her again.

A long time later he tapped at the bedroom door. 'May I come in?' he called. 'I've brought you a glass of sherry.'

'Yes. All right.'

He had brought two glasses and a decanter on a tray, which he put down on the bedside table. The cover on the bed was perfectly smooth, and she was standing at the window with her back to the room, staring out at a frangipani tree that swayed in the breeze. He poured two drinks and handed her one, which she accepted with a quick glance at his carefully expressionless face. Hers was pale but composed, her eyelids slightly pink and heavy. With a painful little tug somewhere in the region of his heart, he thought for the first time since he had known her she looked like a woman, no longer a girl. She also seemed frighteningly remote from him.

She said, 'I'm sorry you found out this way. You didn't deserve that.'

'Drink your sherry,' he said quietly.

She sipped at it, and blinked. 'You've always been so good at looking after me.'

She sounded humbly grateful, and it twisted the knife.

'That was why you were so desperate for a baby,' he said. 'You wanted to replace the one you'd lost.'

'I suppose so,' she said wearily.

'It must be like having a child that died.'

Trista said, 'Yes.' She added almost wonderingly, 'You understand!'

Pierce answered, 'No, I don't suppose I can, fully.

But . . . I've been mourning our baby, too.'

'Oh, Pierce!' she said quickly, her eyes stricken. 'Forgive me! I've been so wrapped up in my own grief . . .'

'It's all right.' He finished his drink. 'How are you feeling now?'

'Tired.'

He reached out to smooth back her hair, feeling the heat of her forehead. 'Want to sleep?'

She nodded, handing him the glass. 'Pierce . . . would you stay with me?' she asked. 'Just . . . stay, I mean, and hold me?'

'Yes,' he agreed. 'Of course.'

He put the glasses on the bedside table, and opened the covers for her. He slipped off his shoes and got in beside her and let her rest her head on his shoulder. For a long time after she slept, he lay staring bleakly at the opposite wall.

She slept right into the morning. Pierce was gone, and when she got up she found him having breakfast.

He looked up, his eyes veiled, and said, 'Feeling better?'

'Yes, thank you.' She had smoothed her hair back and clipped it with a heavy silver clasp. She looked composed and serene, and quite grown-up.

'I have to go to work,' he said. 'Will you be all right?'

'Yes, of course. I'll be fine. I'm sorry I wasn't up in time to make breakfast for you.'

'It doesn't matter. I was getting my own breakfast for years before I married you.'

She cast him a glance that he couldn't fathom, and he wondered if he had said the wrong thing. 'Sit down and have some coffee with me,' he invited.

She obeyed, stirring sugar into her cup with a thoughtful air. 'I might go down to see Antonia,' she said. 'And the children.'

'Today?'

'Yes. Do you mind?'

'Of course not. Drive carefully, won't you? And give Antonia my love . . . and the others.'

Surely it was a good sign, he thought. It had to be . . . didn't it? He wished she would look at him properly. He didn't know what she was thinking . . . feeling. It was like dealing with a different person. Once he had thought he knew Trista. Now he knew a whole lot more about her that he hadn't before . . . and it made her a stranger to him.

She looked no different when he came home that evening, except that she had changed her clothes. He looked at her searchingly, and asked, 'Did you see Antonia?'

'Yes. She's fine, and the new baby's beautiful,' Trista answered without a tremor. 'Kirsten sent something for you, a drawing.'

She went to fetch it, then disappeared into the kitchen. Later she served him a superb meal, and while they ate it she made small-talk, as though she were at one of her father's dinner parties. When she started to get up and take his plate, he stopped her with a hand over hers.

'Trista,' he said.

'Yes?' Again she gave him that frighteningly blank stare.

Pierce shook his head, removing his hand. 'Never mind.'

She gave him a totally meaningless smile, before she resumed the interrupted task and carried his plate off to the kitchen.

Later he tried another way of getting through. She responded passionately to his lovemaking, and he was almost exultant, but afterwards she lay quiet and still, and when he leaned over and brushed a tendril of hair from her cheek he found she was crying.

'Trista! What's the matter? I didn't hurt you, did I?'

'No. Nothing's the matter.' She hunched away from him, pulling the blankets over her shoulders. 'Goodnight.'

He lay back, frowning, until the rhythm of her breathing told him she was asleep.

'I've got a job,' Trista told him the following week. 'I start next Monday.'

'A job?'

'You always said I'd get bored with housework,' she reminded him.

'*Are* you bored?'

She shrugged.

'What kind of job is it?' he asked.

'An office job. It's for a charity; they've just got a computer and they need someone to operate it. It won't pay much, but I'll be doing something useful.'

'A children's charity?' he asked gently.

'No.' Her eyes seemed lifeless. 'Not really. The Family Trust.'

'They do some good work. You'll probably enjoy working for them.'

'Yes.' She gave him a pale travesty of her beautiful smile. 'I hope so.'

He supposed she did enjoy it as much as she enjoyed anything these days. She talked about the place and the people in an impersonal way, with no great enthusiasm, and if anyone asked her about her job she said it was interesting. When Pierce suggested that they should get some help in the house now that they both had jobs to go to, she said, 'It isn't necessary, really. I can cope quite well. It isn't as though we had children.'

Quite sharply, he said, 'Glenda said there's no reason why we shouldn't.'

Trista gave him a smile that seemed almost pitying, and agreed, 'Yes, I know.'

Their lives settled into a new pattern. He lived with a woman he didn't recognise any more. She cooked and cleaned and dressed perfectly as always, though with a new conservatism. And answered his sexual demands with a kind of mechanical passion that baffled him.

'She's not herself,' he said to Charley one day, in an unguarded moment, and felt that it was literally true. 'Sometimes I feel as though there's another person living in her skin.'

'Yes,' Charley sighed. 'I know what you mean. Trista's gone away somewhere and left this—this polite, hollow *alien* in her place. It's weird.'

One day when they were visiting Pierce's parents, Antonia and Ken were there with the children. Pierce watched Trista reading a story to Kirsten and her brother, and quietly nudged Antonia outside with him.

'What do you want?' she asked him. 'It's cold out here!'

'What was Trista like when she came to see you?' he asked. 'The first time she saw the new baby after you brought her home?'

'All right,' Antonia answered. 'Quite OK. I was surprised.'

'What kind of OK?'

Antonia shrugged. 'Well . . . she didn't cry or anything. She asked to see the baby, and said how beautiful she was and . . . you know. Like most people.'

'Trista isn't like most people,' Pierce said. 'Did she seem tense . . . or over-animated, perhaps?'

Antonia shook her head. 'I told you, she was perfectly normal.'

'Did she pick the baby up?'

'Um . . . no. She was asleep most of the time.'

'Like now. Do me a favour, Toni. Make sure that the baby's awake before you go, and *give it to Trista to hold.*'

Antonia stared. 'Pierce, are you sure . . .? I don't know that it's wise to play amateur psychologist.'

'I've got to get through to her, Antonia. Somehow.'

'But surely she's all right, now? She's not depressed any more.'

Pierce groaned. 'You know what she was like before . . . she's nothing like the Trista we used to know.'

'She's . . . different. More mature. But that was bound to happen, Pierce. Losing her baby has hastened the process, that's all.'

'Maybe.' Glenda had said something similar: 'She's starting on a new phase in her life. Sadness does change people. She's picking up well, it's good that she's got a job . . . she's making a good recovery. Give her time.

But he trusted his own and Charley's instincts over Antonia's and Glenda's pragmatism.

Antonia did what he asked, handing the baby casually to Trista to look after while she herded the older two into the car. Pierce watched her face, noticed her quick glance down at the child, and her smile, a quick, intimate, almost secret curve of the lips.

He held his breath, but when Antonia returned Trista handed the child over without a flicker of reluctance, and waved them goodbye with a social smile pinned to her face.

On the way home, he said to her, 'You must have loved him very much.'

'Who?'

Pierce braced himself, looking straight ahead. 'The father of your baby.'

There was quite a lengthy silence. 'Yes, I suppose I did.'

'You *suppose?*'

'All right, yes, I did.'

'What was his name?'

'Chris. Christopher.'

'Christopher what?'

'Does it matter?' she asked, moving restlessly in her seat.

'It might. Tell me.'

'Maddock. Christopher Maddock.'

'Do you know where he is now?'

'No. I don't care.'

Catching the faint note of bitterness in her voice, he said, 'What happened, when he found out you were pregnant? Did he take off?'

'Sort of.'

'What do you mean, sort of?'

She paused for so long that he thought she wasn't going to answer. When at last she did, her voice was light and careless, reminiscent of the old Trista at her most insouciant. 'My father,' she said, 'bought him off.'

CHAPTER TWELVE

'HE *what?*'

'Bought him off. Offered him money to leave the country.' Her lips curved bitterly. 'The temptation was too great to resist. After all, it was what he'd always wanted. He had been saving for a trip overseas.'

'Who told you this?'

'My father. He said it showed what a worthless lot Chris really was.'

'Was he?' Pierce asked carefully.

'Oh, not entirely. At first he offered to marry me if I wanted to keep the baby. Which was noble, because he'd never intended to settle down so soon, although he was hoping I'd come with him when he went overseas. Dad flatly refused to provide a home or any help if I insisted on keeping the baby. He was appalled when I told him I was pregnant. He . . . called me a slut.'

Pierce winced, but said nothing.

'Oh, later he was more understanding . . . kind,' Trista went on. 'But he wanted me to have an abortion. He could have arranged it. He went on so much, so *reasonably*, I almost did, but somehow I held out against that.' She paused, and Pierce glanced at her encouragingly.

'I tried to insist on keeping the baby, but when Chris left I felt so alone and uncertain . . . scared. And when the social worker asked if I thought I could cope in those circumstances, and was it really going to be best thing for the baby, I had to say no.

'Then Dad enlisted Aunt Hester, and she took me on a so-called holiday so that I could have the baby without anyone knowing. It was my last year at school. I left early in the term, and by the time university started the next year . . . it was all over. Aunt Hester was super,' she added. 'She even tried to talk Dad into letting her have the baby. But he said it wouldn't work. The social worker agreed with him. Aunt Hester was too old and didn't have a husband, and they didn't find that type of adoption so good for the child. And . . . whatever else, I did want to do what was best for her, for the baby.'

Pierce nodded. 'But now you're not so convinced it was the right thing?'

'I don't know any more. I suppose . . . it probably was. My father was certain of it. And when he told me Chris had left . . . I gave up then. It didn't seem worth fighting any more. So I signed the adoption papers.'

'A "closed" adoption?'

'Yes. No contact at all. Her . . . parents made it clear that's what they wanted.'

'There's a new law now. She can contact you, if she wants to, when she's grown-up.'

'I know. But she's in Australia. That's where I had her.'

'Don't give up hope,' he said. 'If she wants to see you when she's older, I expect she'll find a way.'

A little later, as they were nearly home, he said, 'I want to apologise to you.'

Surprise brought her eyes to his face. 'Why? What have you done?'

'Just been a smug, condescending male chauvinist. And all the time thinking I was being so sensitive to you, to your needs. You kept telling me you were no child, and I went right on treating you like one. I don't have first-hand experience, but giving birth, I think, certainly qualifies a woman of any age for adulthood.'

She gave a pale imitation of a smile. 'Yes.'

'Did I make it so hard for you to tell me?' he asked.

'You did stop me when I tried,' she acknowledged. 'But I could have made you listen. I owed it to you, I know. Only I was a coward.'

He shook his head. 'A coward you're not. Your father, I suppose, advised against telling me.'

'Yes. I think he was afraid that if you knew, you wouldn't want me at all. He said it was a bit much for any man to accept, and I should forget it ever happened.'

'And then you lost another one,' he said sombrely. 'I'm afraid your father didn't help much there either, did he? I'm sorry, Trista. I let him go on because—well, nothing else seemed to have helped, and I hoped he might get through to you. But telling you to pull yourself out of it wasn't very constructive, I'm afraid.'

'Oh, well, I'm all right now.'

As he drew into their driveway, he said, 'Are you?'

'Of course,' she answered lightly. 'Perfectly.'

As they were going inside, he said, 'Did you mean it, when you said you hated your father?'

'I meant it at the time,' she said. 'But . . . he's my father. I know he loves me in his way. And . . . I love him, too. I suppose he did think it was the best thing.'

'He's certainly concerned about you.'

'Yes. I did apologise for the things I said—and did—that day.'

'I know. He told me.'

Geoffrey had been highly embarrassed about the whole thing when next they met, and obviously apprehensive about Pierce's reaction to the news of Trista's youthful pregnancy. Pierce had cut him off rather curtly, but thought that Geoffrey was nevertheless relieved to hear that he didn't want to discuss the matter.

But now Pierce rather wanted to discuss it. He went round to Geoffrey's house one night on the pretext of asking his advice on a legal matter.

The manufactured query cleared up, Geoffrey gave Pierce an opening by inviting him to have a drink and, when they were both comfortably seated with glasses in their hands, asking, 'And how's that daughter of mine? Don't seem to see much of her these days.'

'Well, you're very busy now, of course,' Pierce said. 'And Trista has a job, too.'

'Mm. Suppose it keeps her from brooding. No sign of another baby yet?'

Pierce shook his head. 'I think Trista's decided in her own mind that she's had all the chances she's going to get, although there's no medical reason to assume that.'

Geoffrey glanced up at the slight emphasis Pierce placed on the word *medical*. 'She's over that depression, isn't she?'

'She seems to be,' Pierce admitted. 'But I'm still worried about her. She's . . . different.'

'In what way?'

'I just can't seem to get through to her. She's not really communicating.'

'You mean she isn't speaking to you?'

'No, I don't mean that. I mean she's—shut herself away. She's lost her sparkle.'

'Quietened down?'

'A lot.'

'Hmm. It was bound to come, you know. She can't

remain a scatty teenager forever.'

A little sharply, Pierce said, 'I wouldn't have called her a scatty teenager at all.'

Geoffrey gave a tolerant little laugh. 'Well, I expect a father can't see his daughter in quite the same light as the man who marries her.'

'I suppose not,' Pierce agreed politely. He took a sip at his glass, and said, 'What happened to Christopher Maddock, do you know?'

'Christopher Maddock?' Geoffrey stared at him in surprise.

'The father of Trista's baby,' Pierce reminded him.

'I know who you mean!' Geoffrey said testily. 'What on earth do you want to know that for?'

Pierce shrugged. 'Natural curiosity. Do you know where he is now?'

'No.' Geoffrey looked at him hard. 'Told you everything, did she?'

'I think so. Where did he live, at the time?'

'Somewhere in Parnell, I think. His father had a garage there. Why?'

'I'm interested. She was in love with the boy. Surely very much in love, back then. It's not so long ago. I suspect she never got over it.'

'Of course she did! There were dozens of boys after that. Not so—so close, of course,' Geoffrey hastily added. 'She'd learned her lesson. But she always had plenty of boyfriends.'

Pierce let that pass. 'She said you bought him off—Chris Maddock.'

Geoffrey grunted, looking at the whisky in his glass before he raised it to gulp down a mouthful.

Something in Pierce's trained lawyer's mind clicked a

warning. 'Is that true?' he pressed.

Geoffrey gave him a half-angry, half-rueful glare, and shrugged. 'Near enough.'

There were times in the courtroom when something, a sixth sense of sorts, told Pierce to pursue a certain question, a train of thought, something that had made the witness in the box suddenly tense, something that might prove to be important, even if he couldn't quite see its significance or where it was leading. He had a strong conviction of it now. Geoffrey was hiding something. He knew it with certainty, just as he knew when a witness was lying.

'Not exactly?' he echoed. 'Then what was it, *exactly?* You *didn't* pay him off?'

Geoffrey shifted uncomfortably in his perfectly comfortable armchair. 'I gave him some money. Look, it's all water under the bridge . . .'

'I want to know, Geoffrey. I need to know.'

'What good——'

'I have a right to know!' Pierce insisted. 'Trista is my wife.' That was an argument that would surely impress his father-in-law.

'Well . . .' Geoffrey said reluctantly, and Pierce began to relax. He waited.

'You have to understand,' Geoffrey said. 'Trista was very young.'

Pierce nodded, with what might have been read as sympathy. He knew better than to interrupt in any way now.

Geoffrey took another sip from his drink and cleared his throat. 'She had this silly, sentimental idea that she wanted to keep the baby, you know. Impossible, of course. She was only a child herself.'

Pierce nodded again.

'Well, as I told you when you got engaged to her, Trista can

be remarkably stubborn. I'd spoken to the boy earlier on——'
His face darkened. 'Young bastard,' he said under his breath.
'Anyway, he kept saying that whatever Trista wanted, he'd be
willing to go along with. Even offered to marry her——no
financial security, of course, no possibility of it. His father was
a garage mechanic, as I just told you, and so far as I could tell
young Maddock's ambitions didn't stretch any further than
hitch-hiking his way around the world.'

Not commenting on the possible difference between a
mechanic and the owner of a business, Pierce murmured, 'I
see.'

'Something had to be done,' Geoffrey said. 'I had to get
Trista to see sense. I told him she'd changed her mind and had
an abortion. That she didn't want to see him any more. Didn't
want to be reminded of the business ever again. He ranted and
yelled a bit, then broke down and cried, and finally took the
cheque I offered him.'

'He *believed* you?'

'I'm a lawyer,' Geoffrey said simply. 'A respected member
of the profession. Of course he believed me.' He added, 'I
don't often lie. But for my daughter . . . and it was all for the
best, in the end.'

'You fool!' Pierce said, after a moment's appalled silence.
'Don't you have any idea what you've done?'

'Done?'

'To Trista!' Pierce said furiously, rising from his chair.
'How could you *do* a thing like that to your own daughter? I
thought you *loved* her!'

Geoffrey got up, too. 'I *do* love her! I've devoted my whole
life to her! How dare you suggest otherwise?'

White-faced, Pierce said loudly, 'Then how could you be so
cruel? You must have seen what it did to her? How it affected
her?'

'She was a perfectly normal, happy girl!' Geoffrey blustered. 'She got over it ——'

'*Over* it? She never got over it! She's still not over it! It's coloured her entire life. When my sister first met her, she said she'd been hurt. I sensed it, too, but I didn't realise how badly, and how gratuitously. And by you! You say you love her. But she was right, you don't understand her, you never have and you never will. I don't believe you've even tried, you *stupid* bloody insensitive—I can't find words for that kind of crassness——'

Geoffrey went red. 'I beg your pardon! I won't stand for th——'

'You should be begging Trista's,' Pierce told him grimly, adding with bitterness, 'but I don't suppose you ever will.'

'You can't talk to me like——'

'Frankly, I'd rather not talk to you at all,' Pierce said, banging his glass down on the table. 'If you'll excuse me, I'll say goodnight.'

It wasn't too difficult to find Chris Maddock. His father still had the business in Parnell, listed in the telephone book.

'Chris is working at Ruakura,' he told Pierce, obviously curious, but too polite to ask why he wanted to know. 'He's studying part-time at the university in Hamilton. Wants to be a researcher.'

Pierce got an address and took an afternoon which he could ill spare away from the office to trace the young man. He didn't want to go down there at the weekend, and have to lie to Trista about his destination.

The Ruakura Agricultural Research Centre just outside Hamilton was a large complex of buildings and green fields devoted to research on all kinds of farming, including soil and plant research. Pierce had to do some fast talking before he was allowed to track down his quarry, who was tending some grapevines that were being grown on specially designed frames to maximise the amount of sun reaching the bunches of fruit.

He was in jeans and a shabby T-shirt, wielding a large pair of secateurs which he transferred to his left hand to shake hands with Pierce in a firm, callused grip.

Pierce, looking at him curiously, saw a tall, thick-set young man several years younger than himself, with an amiable expression but a square, stubborn jaw, who exuded dependability, at the moment looking considerably puzzled. He didn't recognise Pierce's name and was trying to place him. There were a couple of other workers around the vines, but no one close enough to hear the conversation, Pierce noted. They were as private as if they were alone in a room.

'I'm Trista's husband,' he explained briefly.

The young man's blue eyes widened slightly, before a shuttered expression descended on his face. 'How is she?' he asked.

Pierce warmed to him. 'Everyone says she's fine . . . but I'm worried about her.'

Chris frowned quickly. 'Why, what's wrong?'

'I'm not sure. She recently lost a baby. A miscarriage.'

Chris drew in a breath before he said, 'I'm sorry to hear that.' He glanced at Pierce with sympathy. 'I know how you feel.'

Surprised, Pierce said, 'Did you want your baby?'

Chris answered with some relief, 'She told you, then. Yes, I guess I did. Not that we'd planned it, of course. But once it happened—well, I got kind of a kick out of knowing—it's something special, isn't it, making a baby?'

Pierce nodded.

Chris said, 'Only I figured I shouldn't pressure her, you

know? She was the one that'd have to carry it—have it—and in the end, she'd be the one looking after it. Specially since her father refused to help. So I thought, the decision's got to be hers. But I told her if she wanted to keep it, or get married, I'd help as much as I could.' He looked down at the secateurs in his hand, hefting them. 'And in the end,' he said, his voice dropping, 'she decided to . . . get rid of it.'

'No, she didn't,' Pierce told him. 'Her father lied to you, Chris.'

When the blue eyes first lifted to his, they were blank with shock. Then they blazed. The secateurs were flung to the ground. *'Jee—eez!'* Chris swung round, clinging to a rough horizontal branch of the grapevine, his head bent. 'The old bastard! The *bastard*!' The vine shook and rustled.

Pierce gave him a few moments to recover, then said to the broad back, 'You have a daughter. Somewhere in Australia. She was adopted.'

Chris nodded before he turned round. His eyes were moist. 'I believed him,' he said. 'I actually believed it. I felt guilty for letting him talk her into it, because I knew—I thought—he had. I even thought that was one reason why she didn't want me around any more—that she must have thought I'd let her down. I felt rotten about that, too. But I never doubted that it was true. How could I have been so *stupid*?' His head went up as he closed his eyes, fists clenched at his sides.

'Geoffrey would have been very convincing, I should think.' He didn't add that Chris's own patent honesty would have made it easier, especially five years ago, when he must have been no more than twenty.

'Thanks,' Chris said. 'Why are you telling me all this?'

'You loved her didn't you?'

Chris nodded, embarrassed, then suddenly burst out, 'Oh, yes. I loved her. She was the first—and I was for her—well, it's never been like that again.'

Pierce fought down a surge of pure, murderous jealousy. 'She needs to know that,' he said. 'She needs to hear it from you. She thinks that her father bought you off. Paid you to go away.'

A slow flush ascended Chris's cheeks. 'He gave me money. But it wasn't like that.'

'I know.' If Pierce hadn't been sure before, he was now.

'It was . . . after he told me, he was quite nice about it. Said it would be best for both of us—Trista and me—to make a clean break, and she'd be upset if she happened to run into me. He knew I wanted to travel, Trista had mentioned it often. I wanted us to go together, some time. So he said, take this and go, get away from here, away from Trista. And I took it. It seemed the only thing to do, at the time . . . I paid him back later, though. When I got back. Sent it to him in cash.'

'But never saw Trista?'

Chris shook his head, his jaw very prominent. 'I'd promised I wouldn't.'

'Has there been someone else since?' Pierce asked him.

'Not now. There've been other girls. No one serious.'

Pierce said carefully, 'How do you feel about Trista now?'

Chris thought. 'I don't know,' he admitted. 'A memory. I've . . . not really thought about her for ages. Not the way I used to.'

'Will you see her?' Pierce asked. 'Talk to her?'

'You mean, explain what happened?'

'Why you went away, yes.'

'You think that will help?'

'I hope so,' Pierce said. 'I'm desperate.'

'You must love her very much,' Chris said slowly.

Pierce said, 'That isn't important.'

Chris gave a slight, disbelieving shake of his blond head.

'Not important?'

'Only to me.'

'It must be important to her,' Chris commented doggedly.

Pierce gave a slight, wry smile. 'What she needs,' he said, 'is to know that *you* loved her. At the moment she feels nothing for me . . . or for anyone, I suspect. And it goes back to the fact that she thinks you . . . betrayed her.'

Chris shook his head sorrowfully. 'I guess I did. Maybe, deep down, I wanted to believe her father—have the responsibility taken out of my hands. I hadn't meant to be tied down to a family, you know. So—it was kind of a relief, even though I . . . oh, I don't know, I was all mixed up.' He looked again at Pierce. 'If she doesn't love you, why did Trista marry you?'

Pierce said frankly, 'Partly, it was because I didn't fall at her feet and worship her like all the other men she knew. She found that a challenge. It . . . made me more attractive to her.' *Turned her on*, he thought bleakly, but couldn't bring himself to use the phrase aloud. 'But mostly, I've realised, because she was desperate to have a baby, to replace the one she'd lost by having it adopted.'

Chris said with respect, 'You're quite a bloke.'

Brushing that aside, Pierce asked, 'Will you see her?'

'You want me to visit you?'

'I don't know that I want to be there, but basically, yes.'

Chris rubbed a finger over his upper lip, dipped his head, then raised it again. 'OK.'

CHAPTER THIRTEEN

PIERCE made sure that Trista would be home the following weekend. She said to him once, 'What's the matter?' And he turned a bland face to her and denied that anything was.

But he had been restless, prowling to the window and away again, not able to settle to anything. In the end, he went outside and began trimming some of the big shrubs in the garden, although the day was blustery and unpleasant.

When at last a red car slowed and turned into the drive, he straightened and dropped the pruning saw he had been using.

The car drove on to the small sealed parking area beside the double garage. Chris got out and deliberately closed the car door. He stood looking at the house, and Pierce, with a heavy sense of foreboding in his chest, took a deep breath and went over to meet him.

Chris held out his hand, and briefly Pierce put his into it. 'She's inside,' he said, and led the way.

They went in the front door. He could hear Trista doing something in the kitchen. 'I'll fetch her,' he said. 'Wait in here.' Politely he pushed wide the door of the lounge and Chris walked in. 'Sit down,' Pierce said, but Chris stood in the middle of the room, facing him, and silently shook his head.

Pierce walked down the short passageway to the kitchen, feeling as though he was on his way to his execution. A small, traitorous voice inside urged him to go back, send

Chris away again before Trista found out he was here. He set his teeth and kept walking.

'There's someone here to see you,' he said, surprised that his voice sounded steady, quite casual.

She turned from the sink with a cleaning cloth in her hand, and raised the fingers of the other to brush back a stray wisp of hair. His heart turned like a knife in his chest. 'Who?'

His throat closing, Pierce managed a shrug.

Trista put down the cloth, and rinsed her hands, drying them on the apron she wore before taking it off.

He stood aside for her and was behind her when she stopped dead in the doorway of the lounge. Chris hadn't moved.

Pierce saw how still she was, and counted the seconds. At last she said, her voice catching huskily, 'Chris?' And then, on a quite different, vibrant note, '*Chris!*'

Pierce saw the movement of Chris's throat as he swallowed, before his hands came up and he held them out to her, and Trista's hands went out to meet them as she stepped into the room.

Pierce turned away and seconds later found himself in the bedroom, staring out of the window. He looked at his hands and saw that they were grimy. After a moment he went to the bathroom and washed them. A murmur of voices came from the lounge. He closed his eyes, leaning on the basin, his forehead against the coolness of the mirror above.

He raised his head, saw his own face looking gaunt and white, a tight look about the mouth. He passed a hand across his forehead, squeezing his suddenly throbbing temples.

His car keys hung on a rack by the back door. Quietly he walked down the passageway and collected them, then let himself out by the back door. In the garage he kept his eyes averted from Trista's car and got into his own, and carefully reversed on to the road.

*   *   *

He drove, and then walked, and two hours later got back into his car and went home. Chris's car was gone from the car park, and the garage was empty.

He found the back door locked, and used his key with a strong sense of fatalism. In the bedroom, Trista's brush and comb and the little bottles that usually stood on the dressing-table were gone. There were still a lot of clothes in the wardrobe, but he counted six empty hangers, and her drawers were untidy, as though she had pulled things out in a hurry. She had taken her toothbrush and the bottle of bath salts he had given her for Christmas from the bathroom, the capacious leather handbag she always used, and the satin robe that always hung on the inside of her wardrobe door. He pictured her in it, the pearl-like fabric clinging to her as she slung back her loose hair after a bath—pictured Chris Maddock with her, and flung himself down on the bed, his hand over his eyes.

Two days later a postcard came, postmarked Hamilton. Incongruously, it had a picture of Garden Place on the front, the flowers in full bloom. On it she had scrawled, 'Don't worry about me. I'm all right.'

And not even her name. Nothing else but the terse reassurance.

He wondered if she had contacted Geoffrey, and thought probably not. He stood looking at the card, then took it inside and sat on one of the chairs in the lounge with it in his hands. 'Be happy,' he murmured, and dropped his head on his clenched hands, the card crushed in his fingers.

Inevitably, of course, he had to tell his family, and Geoffrey. To his parents and his sisters, he said that Trista had left him, and he didn't want to talk about it. Mercifully, even Charley managed to respect that wish. He knew they were shocked, but all they expressed to him was sympathy. He was afraid that Antonia, living close to Hamilton herself, might bump into Trista, perhaps in Chris's company, but if she did she kept that to herself, and he was grateful.

Geoffrey, mercifully, seemed to be concentrating on his judicial duties and had not been in touch. Mortally offended, Pierce supposed, after that confrontation and Pierce's angry reaction to his revelations. But he felt obliged, in the end, to go and see him.

Geoffrey greeted him stiffly and didn't offer a drink, but did invite him to sit down.

It was going to be a difficult interview, Pierce realised. Well, he had not expected anything else. He apologised briefly for losing his temper at their last meeting. If Geoffrey noticed that he wasn't apologising for what he had said, he didn't say so.

'All right,' he grunted. Then, 'How is Trista?'

Pierce mentally took a deep breath. 'She's with Chris Maddock.'

It was several minutes before Geoffrey could bring himself to speak. His face swelled with rage and shock, and his eyes showed whitely. '*How?*' he said finally. 'How could you *let* her? Good lord, Pierce, I never took you for a fool!'

Pierce smiled faintly. 'Perhaps I am. How and why doesn't really matter, does it? I thought you should know, though.'

'I can't believe this!' Geoffrey muttered, shaking his head. 'I just can't believe it.'

'I'm afraid it's true. I expect she'll contact you eventually. When she feels more . . . settled.'

'Settled? She can't settle with that . . . She'll come back, Pierce, I'm sure she will. She thinks the world of you, really. It's a temporary aberration. She's still depressed, ill, you said she's not back to her normal self. Well, obviously you were right.'

Pierce shook his head. 'I wouldn't count on that.'

Geoffrey frowned. 'Are you saying you wouldn't take her back?'

'I'm not saying that. But I am saying, she should be allowed to choose what she wants—and who she wants.'

Geoffrey gave a scornful snort. 'She doesn't know what she wants! She's got another of her wild impulses, that's all. Going off with a childhood sweetheart! Where are they, do you know? I might be able to talk some sense into her——'

'No, Geoffrey,' Pierce said firmly. 'She's over twenty-one, and you're not responsible for her any longer. Neither am I.'

'Nonsense! As her husband——'

'I can't tell her what to do. I'm certainly not about to go and drag her back by the hair.'

Geoffrey scowled. 'Don't you want her any more?'

'Oh, yes,' Pierce said softly. 'I want her.'

Geoffrey averted his eyes from Pierce's face, clearing his throat, 'I don't understand you,' he said gruffly.

'Are you sure Trista's all right?' Charley asked him one day when she had come to visit. She came rather often these days, which touched him. Tactfully, this was the first time she had directly mentioned Trista. 'She hasn't written to me or anything, and we are—we *were*—friends.'

'You're also my sister,' Pierce reminded her. 'I had a postcard,' he said, and showed the crumpled object to her.

She handed it back. 'That's OK, I suppose. But it was quite a while ago, wasn't it?'

'A few weeks,' he said. 'Nearly a month.' It seemed like an age. 'I could check, I suppose,' he added almost to himself, wondering if he was seizing on a tempting excuse to contact his wayward bride.

'You know where she is, then?' Charley asked on a note

of relief.

'Yes, I know where she is. And before you ask, I won't give you the address. If she wants to get in touch with you, she will.'

'I wouldn't have asked,' Charley said reproachfully, and he smiled at her and apologised.

The suggestion lodged in his mind and niggled at him all week. He had Chris Maddock's home address in Hamilton, and the telephone number, but he wouldn't ring there, in case . . . in case Trista answered. Because he couldn't have borne to hear her voice on the phone without begging her to come home, he knew. But dammit, she was his wife, he thought, working himself up to a temper. He had a right to enquire after her well-being, and she hadn't bothered to contact him after that one brief message on a postcard . . .

He phoned the research station, and had to leave a message because Chris was out in the field somewhere. He tried to concentrate on what he was doing for the next hour, but every time the phone on his desk shrilled he pounced on it. When at last he heard his secretary say, 'A Mr Maddock on the line—will you speak to him?' he barked,

'Yes!'

'You wanted me?' Chris asked.

Pierce swallowed and sat back in his chair, his hand slippery on the receiver. 'I just wondered,' he said. 'I don't want to interfere, but I'd like to know how Trista is.'

'Trista?'

Pierce clamped his teeth tight for a moment. 'Just tell me if she's all right,' he said patiently. 'That's all. And I won't bother you again.'

There was a silence on the other end. Then Chris said in puzzled tones, 'I haven't seen Trista since that day at your house. We talked for about half an hour, then I left.' He paused again. 'You thought she was with *me?*'

Pierce, shocked into a state of hollow panic, said, 'I was sure she was with you! I had a postcard from Hamilton.'

'Nothing to do with me, mate. When was this?'

'A couple of days later,' Pierce said. 'I thought she'd left with you—she took her car, but I assumed she'd followed you.'

'You mean, she's been gone since then? Since the day I came?'

'Yes.' Visions of accident, suicide, of Trista wandering in the dark streets of some strange city screamed through Pierce's mind. 'How was she when you left?' he demanded. 'What did you say?'

'I told her what had happened. That's all. Told her I—how I felt about her, at the time—why I went away. Just what you suggested. She thanked me, we parted. End of story.'

'That's all?'

Chris cleared his throat. 'We kissed—like a brother and sister, I swear. There was nothing . . . I mean, she was just the same when I left as when I arrived. A little more . . . relaxed, maybe. As though she had decided something.'

'Didn't you want her? Pierce asked harshly. 'Did you reject her *again?*'

'Look, the question didn't arise,' Chris said, sounding slightly harassed. 'Honestly. She's changed—we both have, I guess. It was . . . strange, seeing each other again, but it was a bit as though all that happened before had happened to two other people, you know? She was glad to see me, at first, as she might be glad to see any old friend. But something's gone. Whatever we had before . . . it's died.'

'Maybe not for her,' Pierce suggested.

'For both of us. Her more than me,' Chris insisted. 'She's still gorgeous, and if she were free I could fall for her all over again. But I know it wasn't there for her, believe me.'

'Then *why?*' Pierce said. 'And for pity's sake, where?'

'I haven't a clue,' Chris answered, nonplussed. 'You know her better than I do.'

What now? Pierce asked himself, after hanging up. And where? Where did he start looking?

She hadn't left an address book, and the few numbers scribbled on the notepad by the phone yielded no clues. He phoned the office where she had worked, and they said she had contacted them, told them she was sorry but she had been called away unexpectedly and wouldn't be back.

'Did she leave a forwarding address?' he asked, not caring that they would know she had left him, not knowing if they were telling the truth when they said no. She had asked them to keep her wages in lieu of notice, to compensate for the inconvenience. That started him wondering what she was doing for money. She had not taken her cheque-book. A few days before that weekend she had cashed a cheque for a hundred dollars, but he didn't know if she had any other cash, or how much of that she might have already spent.

Geoffrey. Geoffrey must know something, have some addresses for her friends. Her second bridesmaid, for instance, had lived in Wellington.

But Geoffrey, livid at the new turn of events and blaming Pierce almost as much as he blamed himself, drew a blank too.

'Can't find a thing,' he announced, after turning out Trista's old room.

'Has she phoned Hester at all? Written to her?'

'No. I've asked Hester.'

'Names,' Pierce said. 'Write down any names you can recall, anyway. Some will be in the phone book, surely. Ring them.' A cold thought struck him. 'Did she have a passport?' Five years ago, had New Zealanders required passports to get into Australia? He couldn't remember.

'I've still got that. And she can't get another without her birth certificate. I've got that, too.'

At least she couldn't have left the country. Small mercies, Pierce thought.

Charley. She might have talked to Charley about her other friends. About places she had been, places she might have returned to now. The other bridesmaid, of course!

'Sorry,' Charley said, after an exhaustive search through her memory banks. 'Can't recall that she ever mentioned the address. And she was flatting with a crowd, so I don't suppose the phone will be in her name.'

'You're sure of her name, though?'

'Sure. Brenda Thwaites.'

'It's a start,' Pierce muttered. 'I'll have to hire a detective.'

'She might not like that.'

'What she likes or doesn't hardly matters, does it?' he said forcefully, making her blink. 'She might be in danger, Charley! She's got very little money . . . she could be lost . . . what if she decided to hitch-hike or something idiotic like that?'

'She's a grown woman, Pierce! I'm sure Trista's capable of looking after herself. She's not stupid. Stop panicking.'

'She's . . .' He stopped. 'You're right. It's just that . . . I thought I knew where she was, who she was with, and I trusted him. But now——'

Charley's eyes had widened a little at the 'him' he had let slip, but it was a few moments before she said, 'Pierce, it's none of my business, I suppose, but I can't understand why she left.'

'Neither can I, now.'

'What do you mean?'

He sighed. 'I thought she'd gone to another man, but I was apparently wrong. Unless . . . unless she does want him, but can't quite bring herself to be physically unfaithful on principle.'

Charley said, 'You're crazy!'

'Probably,' Pierce agreed gloomily. 'I certainly feel punch-drunk these days.'

'Whatever,' Charley said. 'If you think Trista would look at someone else, you've got to be round the bend. The girl is *besotted* with you.'

Pierce shook his head wearily. 'I don't know where you got that idea from——'

Charley snorted. 'Anyone who saw the way she *looked* at you could have told you that! Didn't you even *notice?*'

'Of course I noticed. Trista has a way of making any man think he is the only one in the world . . . at least she did . . . until . . .'

'I don't mean that!' Charley said impatiently. 'That's a different sort of look altogether—her vamp act. Besides, she said enough to give me the picture. Pierce, for Trista there *is* no other man in the world.'

'I can't believe that,' he said impatiently.

Charley raised her eyes to the ceiling. 'Pierce! Modesty is all very well, but you carry it to extremes. I'm telling you, Trista loves you! I *know* what I'm talking about. If you ask me, she probably left because she's convinced you don't feel the same way about her.'

'That's——' Prepared to deny it, Pierce stopped short.

'Well?' Charley demanded. '*Do* you love her?'

'Of course I love Trista!' Pierce passed a hand over his hair, scowling.

'Thank goodness for that,' Charley said crisply. 'Have you told her that lately?'

Pierce, still frowning heavily, muttered, 'I haven't told her at all.'

'*Pierce!*' Charley wailed in dismay. 'Why the *hell* not?'

'At first,' he confessed, 'because I was afraid. And then—because I didn't think it mattered to her, anyway.'

Charley threw up her hands in despair. '*Men!* What on earth gave you the idea that it didn't matter? And what do you mean, *afraid?*'

Defensively, Pierce said, 'I told you when I first met her what Trista was like then.'

'Eating men for breakfast,' Charley nodded. 'But not you.'

'No, not me. Because I was different. I wouldn't—succumb. Not obviously, anyway. Trista was into power games with men—I've only recently found out why. But I didn't dare let her get under my guard.'

'But you asked her to marry you.'

He smiled slightly. 'No. Actually Trista did that—asked *me*.'

Charley gaped, then grinned. 'I can imagine that,' she said appreciatively. 'She has guts.'

'Yes. She has. Well, it let me out nicely. She thought that I went along with it because she was Geoffrey's daughter.'

Charley shook her head. 'I didn't know you were such a stinker,' she said sorrowfully.

'A safe stinker,' he agreed ruefully. 'A very wary stinker. I thought maybe she was beginning to really love me, but I was still not game to risk letting her know how I felt, take the suspense out of the relationship for her, in case it lost its flavour. Then . . . the baby happened, and everything changed afterwards.'

'Yes, I know. Trista changed.'

'I even gave up making love to her, in the end,' Pierce admitted, looking away from her.

'Oh, that would be a great help!' Charley guessed sarcastically.

'You don't know what it was like,' Pierce said. 'I felt that it was just another of the wifely duties she carried out so damned efficiently.'

'What, close your eyes and think of England?' Charley said.

'No. More . . . efficient than that. But worse. Making the right responses, but with no heart in it. The way she did everything, these last few months.'

Charley shook her head, allowing him a moment of sympathy. 'How awful.'

'Yes, it was.'

'I think you should have told her,' Charley suggested, 'that you loved her. It might have helped.'

'If you're right,' he said, 'it might have been the only thing that would have helped.'

'I'm right!' She walked over and gave his arm a little shake. 'You men can be so thick, sometimes. You're arrogant and bossy at all the wrong times, and then ridiculously unsure of yourselves when a bit of self-confidence is just what you need.'

Pierce's detective found the bridesmaid in Wellington, and confirmed that Trista had stayed there, but moved out. He didn't have her home address, but she was working for a computer company in the city.

'Thank heaven,' Pierce breathed, and picked up the phone to assure Geoffrey that his daughter was safe. 'I'm flying down on the first available plane,' he said, hoping Keita would forgive him for offloading his paperwork on to her.

'And bringing her home, I hope,' Geoffrey growled.

'I hope so, too,' Pierce said fervently.

She was coming out of the big building when he stepped in front of her, blocking her path. She looked thin, he thought, and fine-boned, but still achingly beautiful. Her eyes seemed larger, or perhaps it was just the way she was looking at him.

She made to walk round him, and he moved closer, grabbing at her arm. There were people hurrying past them, casting curious or impatient glances their way.

'No,' Trista said in a small voice, and bent her head until it almost touched his lapel.

'Yes, Trista—please,' he said. 'We have to talk.'

She sighed in defeat and said, 'All right.'

'Where do you live? Can we go there? Do you bring your car to work?' And, when she shook her head, 'I'll get a taxi.'

It was a very small flat, dark but clean. There was a kitchen and a bathroom, and one room containing a wide divan-bed half covered in a variety of cushions, a rather hard, wooden-armed armchair, and a small drop-leaf table with two dining chairs that didn't match.

'I can't afford much,' she said. 'But they've promised me a rise in six months.'

Six months? He let that pass, sitting down on the easy chair she offered him.

'Would you like a cup of coffee?' she asked.

Pierce shook his head. She was taking off the jacket she wore, hanging it on a hook behind the door. There was another hook there, holding her satin gown. He looked at it, remembering.

She turned, flushing as she met his naked eyes.

'I want you,' he said truthfully, hearing the starkness of his own voice with a small shock.

Trista shivered, and backed against the door, her hands flattened on the wood, her head turned to one side as she closed her eyes.

He got up and crossed the small space, turned her face to him almost angrily, and covered her mouth in a kiss of possession, smothering her attempt at protest.

He felt her shudder, and then her mouth opened for him,

and he knew a quick surge of triumph. He drew back, breathing hard. They had established something, at least. His satisfaction showed in his face.

'Have you got anything stronger than coffee?' he asked her.

She looked dazed. 'Sherry,' she said.

'That'll do.'

He took the bottle from her and poured two glasses. He was putting down the bottle on the tiny bench when she said suddenly, 'You can't *do* this to me! It isn't fair!'

'Do what?'

'Change your mind!' she said, gesturing a little wildly.

'About?' he asked politely.

'About wanting me! I know why you sent Chris to me. Went to all the trouble of finding him.'

'Do you? I hoped you would.' He handed her a glass of sherry, and then, as he saw the sudden flash in her eyes, said quickly in warning, 'No, don't throw it at me.'

She took a gulp of it instead, and almost choked. Pierce took up the other glass and regarded her over it. 'Well?' he invited gently.

'I'm sorry your plans went awry, but I'm not a parcel to be handed on when you tire of me,' she said, turning away. 'And you didn't need to provide me with—compensation, or whatever that was supposed to be.'

Pierce put his untouched glass back on the bench. 'What?'

Recklessly, she drank some more and swung round to face him again across the room. 'It was a kind thought. But if you wanted to get rid of me, you had only to say so. Or were you anxious to ensure that I was the guilty party so that my father couldn't blame you for breaking up our marriage, and your career would still be safe?'

Pierce blinked at her, and, as he understood, was consumed by a white flare of pure rage. He started towards her, and she flung the almost empty glass, her face suddenly taut with fright, but he sidestepped it and grasped her shoulders in a bruising grip.

He was within an ace of shaking her, but her wide, scared eyes stopped him. He dropped his hands and said grittily, as he pushed her towards the divan, 'Sit down!'

Her head came up defiantly, but at the look in his eyes she subsided on to the mattress.

He said, 'I don't know how you got the idea that I was tired of you! It seemed to me that *you* had lost interest in being married and were just going through the motions because you felt obliged to stick it out. And I wasn't *handing you over*. I hoped against hope that you wouldn't go with Chris, but it was a risk I had to take. When I came home and found you gone, I assumed that was what you had done. You sent a postcard from Hamilton, for heaven's sake!'

'I stopped there for petrol,' she said, 'on the way to Wellington. What does that have to do with anything?'

'Chris lives there!'

'Oh. Does he? I don't think he mentioned it.'

'And I *never* wanted to be rid of you. I thought that seeing him, hearing what he had to say, might have helped you out of that—fog you were living in.'

She raised her eyes. 'You knew?'

'I knew. How could I not know?'

'I tried . . . to hide it. To act like a normal human being.'

'I know that, too. You're not a normal human being . . . not an average human being, anyway. You're a wonderful, unique, very beautiful woman. With something special about you that very few people can match. And it broke my heart to see you lose that.'

Disregarding her astonished stare, he turned and picked up the glass from where it had rolled, refilled it and brought it back with his. 'Move over,' he said. 'We've got some sorting out to do.'

He put his arm about her, and pulled her back against him, settling against the cushions. 'Drink your sherry,' he said. 'After Chris went away—after you had his baby, your father thought you'd got over it. But you hadn't.' When she remained silent, his arm folded her closer, and he brushed a kiss against her temple. 'Had you?' he asked.

She sighed. 'I did, but there were things that I found . . . difficult. I used to keep away from babies—young children. When my friends got married and started families, I stopped seeing them. I made the excuse to myself that our interests had separated, that we had nothing in common any more.'

'And meantime you concentrated on punishing all the young men of your acquaintance for Chris's defection and your father's . . . bullying.'

She was silent for a while, taking sips of her drink. 'I . . . didn't think of it like that,' she said at last. 'I thought I was just having a good time, taking Dad's advice.'

'What advice?'

'"Get out and about. Don't moon about the house thinking about it, put it all behind you, and for goodness' sake stop showing me that long face." He hates to see me cry.'

'So you stuck a smile on your face and went out to have a good time. And tried to pretend nothing had happened.'

'Yes. And it did work . . . up to a point. I had fun.'

'When you danced . . .' Pierce mused.

'I let the music come inside me, and it filled up the space . . . for a while.'

'And sex?'

'Once bitten . . .' she said. 'Oh, kissing . . . even petting, occasionally. Yes, I tried that. But I didn't want sex again, really. Until I met you. And then . . . you introduced me to the

McGregors, and Jennifer. And Kirsten. Kirsten would be about the same age, you see . . .'

'In that order?' Pierce said slowly. He reached over and put his glass on the floor.

'What order?'

'You said, you didn't want sex until you met me. And *then* I introduced you to Jennifer and Kirsten.'

She looked down at the teaspoonful of amber liquid left in her glass. 'Why did you marry me, Pierce?'

Without hesitation he said, 'Because I love you. Because you're the only woman I've wanted to love and to cherish all the days of my life. Because I can't imagine life without you.'

Her voice low, she said, 'You've never said that before.'

'I love you? No, I haven't. And many a time I've bitten my tongue, trying to stop it from escaping.' He added deliberately, 'I didn't quite dare. Because I wasn't sure why you married me . . . and there was only reason that was . . . safe.'

'Take this glass,' she said, handing it to him. When he had deposited it beside his own, she propped herself on her elbow, with one hand on his chest, and said, 'I didn't marry you just to have babies. I was in love with you almost from the moment we met. Only, I thought half of the attraction for you was my father's influence, and the fact that he had more or less pushed you to take an interest in me.'

'I'm not so easily pushed.' He lifted a tendril of hair away from her cheek, hooking it behind her ear. 'It bothered you, didn't it? That I might not have married you if you hadn't had a useful father.'

'I was . . . disappointed. Which was really stupid. I'd have been devastated if you hadn't agreed to marry me.'

'So you were in a cleft stick. I could have spanked you several times during our engagement . . . if I'd been the type,' he added hastily as she gave him a straight look. 'Some of those sweet-but-cutting remarks were a bit near the bone.'

'You didn't trust me.'

'Not an inch,' he admitted with a wry grin. 'I didn't know why you were "agin" all men, but I had a suspicion that once you knew you had me wound about your little finger, I'd end up like all the rest—on a plate. And I wasn't about to risk my skin.'

She made a face at him, and dropped her head to his shoulder. The ache about his heart began to ease. She wasn't the spoiled adolescent he had thought her, and he wouldn't be making that mistake again. But even adults were allowed their moments of playfulness, and he had missed such childish gestures when they suddenly disappeared. They had been pure Trista. So was the way she was now fiddling with the button on his shirt. He let her undo two of them, then picked up her hand and began nibbling gently on her fingers. 'Shall I tell you something?' he said. 'If you'd waited about another five minutes, that day by the river, I'd have proposed to *you*.'

She looked up at him. 'Oh! Well, I couldn't wait.' She dropped her mouth to his neck, nuzzling his skin.

Pierce took her shoulders and rolled over, pinning her beneath him, admiring her flawless face.

'Do you want to make another baby?' he asked her.

Trista gave him a slow, languorous smile. 'That would be nice,' she said, stretching her arms over her head. 'But somehow it doesn't seem quite so important now. I think . . . I was kind of obsessed with the idea, when I wasn't sure you loved me. A baby would have bound you to me.'

'You don't need a baby for that,' he said. 'I'm bound to you hand and foot, heart and soul, forever. But I'm sure there will be babies eventually. Children of our love.'

She wound her arms about his neck. 'Yes,' she whispered. 'Oh, yes. There will. Tell me again that you love me, Pierce.'

He told her again. And again. Until he was too breathless to speak, and she too intoxicated with pleasure to hear.

When it was over, he held her and stroked her, and she sighed against him.

'Happy?' he asked.

'I don't remember being so happy in my life,' she answered drowsily. 'I never thought you'd come after me. Would you have, if I'd been with Chris?'

'Not while I thought you were happier with him.'

She confessed, 'I couldn't imagine that you would have let me go, if you loved me.'

'*Because* I love you.'

'I don't know what I'll do if you ever leave me, Pierce.'

'I won't,' he promised.

Trista snuggled closer and closed her eyes.

'Don't go to sleep yet,' he said. 'I've put myself completely in your power. It's your turn. Be brave.'

She frowned, puzzled for a moment. Then she raised her head a little and feathered a tiny kiss against his cheek. 'I love you,' she whispered, and settled down again on his chest, and slept.

Harlequin Presents®

Coming Next Month

Have You Ever Wondered If You Could Write A Harlequin Novel?

Here's great news—Harlequin is offering a series of cassette tapes to help you do just that. Written by Harlequin editors, these tapes give practical advice on how to make your characters—and your story—come alive. There's a tape for each contemporary romance series Harlequin publishes.

Mail order only

All sales final

TO: *Harlequin Reader Service*
Audiocassette Tape Offer
P.O. Box 1396
Buffalo, NY   14269-1396

I enclose a check/money order payable to HARLEQUIN READER SERVICE® for $9.70 ($8.95 plus 75¢ postage and handling) for EACH tape ordered for the total sum of $_____*
Please send:

☐ Romance and Presents   ☐ Intrigue
☐ American Romance   ☐ Temptation
☐ Superromance   ☐ All five tapes ($38.80 total)

Signature_____
                                                    (please print clearly)
Name:_____

Address:_____

State:_____ Zip:_____

*Iowa and New York residents add appropriate sales tax.

                                                    AUDIO-H

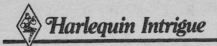

Harlequin Intrigue

Two exciting new stories each month.

Each title mixes a contemporary, sophisticated romance with the surprising twists and turns of a puzzler...romance with "something more."

Because romance can be quite an adventure.

Intrg-1

Romance, Suspense and Adventure